IN THE BOARDROOM

Greek tycoons become devoted dads!

The Andreas brothers were born with success in
their blood.... Hardworking and at the top of their
game, they're all-about-the-money kind of guys
who think business, not babies. That is, until now!

*Because when babies arrive in the boardroom,
work is going to be the last thing
on these tycoons' minds!*

Don't miss any of the fabulous stories
in Susan Meier's brand-new trilogy:

The Baby Project—April 2011
Second Chance Baby—May 2011
Baby on the Ranch—June 2011

Dear Reader,

Every once in a while in a writer's career a really great story idea comes along. For me, *The Baby Project* was one of those ideas.

With the loss of both her husband and baby daughter, Whitney Ross had suffered the kind of tragedy most of us will never experience. But Darius hadn't had an easy life either. Imagine, not merely being ignored by your super-rich father, but also discovering that you had three half brothers. One of them a baby!

When Darius and Whitney are named Gino's guardians, neither expects to be overwhelmingly attracted. Still, both are positive they're strong enough to handle it and each other.

But raising a baby and falling in love are equally surprising. Sometimes funny. Sometimes poignant. Darius and Whitney discover that when everything seems to be rolling out of control, the best idea is to simply hang on.

Join us for the laughter and the tears when Darius and Whitney try to raise little Gino, form a family with Darius's two cantankerous adult half brothers and unexpectedly fall desperately, breathlessly in love.

Susan Meier

P.S. Look for Nick's story, *Second Chance Baby,* in May and Cade's story, *Baby on the Ranch,* in June!

SUSAN MEIER

The Baby Project

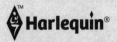

TORONTO NEW YORK LONDON
AMSTERDAM PARIS SYDNEY HAMBURG
STOCKHOLM ATHENS TOKYO MILAN MADRID
PRAGUE WARSAW BUDAPEST AUCKLAND

Recycling programs
for this product may
not exist in your area.

ISBN-13: 978-0-373-74090-1

THE BABY PROJECT

First North American Publication 2011

Susan Meier spent most of her twenties thinking she was a job-hopper—until she began to write and realized everything that had come before was only research! One of eleven children, with twenty-four nieces and nephews and three kids of her own, Susan has had plenty of real-life experience watching romance blossom in unexpected ways. She lives in western Pennsylvania with her wonderful husband, Mike, three children and two overfed, well-cuddled cats, Sophie and Fluffy. You can visit Susan's website at www.susanmeier.com.

CHAPTER ONE

"THE ANDREAS BROTHERS have arrived."

As the secretary's announcement came through the speaker phone, attorney Whitney Ross turned from the window in her father's law office. The gathering January storm clouds above the New York City skyscrapers concerned her, but the Andreas brothers' visit would be every bit as tumultuous.

Gerard Ross pressed a button on his phone. "Tell them I need five minutes."

"You're enjoying this."

"Not *enjoying* exactly." He grimaced, leaning his round body back in his office chair. He rhythmically tapped the blotter on his cherrywood desk. "How about if we say Stephone used his will to accomplish a few important things?"

Though Whitney had never met Stephone Andreas's sons, the man had been a close friend of her father's. He'd come to dinner at least once a month from the time she was six, and had talked about "his boys" incessantly. So she suspected she knew what was going on. The senior Andreas had always believed his three sons needed a kick in the pants and it seemed he'd finally found a way to give them one.

"You persuaded Stephone to use his will to force them to grow up."

"This is about more than growing up. All three are smart. All three are good business-men. Any one of them could take over the family holdings. But not one of them has a sense of loyalty or family."

"And this is where the will comes in?"

"Yes. Stephone made his oldest son, Darius, chairman and CEO and left him the Montauk estate. Whether that divides them for good or forces them to unite all depends on whether Darius takes the reins like a true leader."

He rose and headed for the black leather sofa in the comfortable meeting area in the corner of his big law office. After he sat, he patted the spot beside him, indicating that it was where Whitney should sit for their up-coming meeting.

"But before I bring the brothers in, there's something you need to know. Missy had something put in her will for you that Stephone agreed would also go into his."

Whitney took the seat he'd offered. "Missy put something in her will for me?" She wasn't surprised. Missy Harrington had been her roommate from the time they were freshman at university the whole way through law school. With an alcoholic mom and a dad who'd left when Missy was young, Missy had adopted Whitney's family as her own, and they in turn had taken her under their wing. For seven years she'd shared every holiday and most of her vacations with the Rosses. Whitney had hardly seen Missy since she had introduced her friend to Stephone Andreas, but they had still shared a strong bond.

"She didn't exactly leave you something. In accordance with Stephone's and Missy's wills, you and Darius got shared custody of their son."

Whitney's stomach squeezed. "What?"

"Okay. Look. It's been three years since the accident that took Burn and Layla. And though I had never dreamed that Missy and Stephone would die so soon when I let them put this provision in their wills, it's still time you came back to the land of the living." Her dad pulled a small envelope from one of the files in the stack on the coffee table. "She left this note for you."

Whitney wrapped her hand around the envelope, and she paled.

"In the unlikely event of their deaths, Stephone wanted Darius to raise their son, but Missy was adamant about you having joint custody. The Andreas brothers are rich and spoiled. And they don't even know their father had another son. It's anybody's guess how they'll react when they find out. I believe that Missy made you co-guardian to ensure that Gino was also in the hands of someone *she* knew could take the reins and care for her baby."

"But I don't know Gino! When Missy and Stephone moved to Greece, we practically lost touch. I've never even met Gino. I'll be no better for this baby than his brother."

He caught her hand. "You might not know Gino, but Missy knew you. She knew you had a sense of family. A sense of right and wrong. You've also been a mom. You'll get to know Gino and, as young as he is, Gino will grow accustomed to you, too." He squeezed her fingers. "Besides, you need this."

She tried to bounce off the sofa, but her dad held fast to her hand. When she faced him her eyes were blazing. "No! I don't *need* this! I'm fine!"

"You're not fine. Otherwise, getting custody of Gino wouldn't make you angry."

He pressed a button on the phone on the coffee table that sat in the center of the circle made by the sofa and three black leather chairs. "Cynthia, bring in Gino, please."

Whitney's heart stopped. Her stomach rolled. Her head spun. For the past three years she'd avoided even being near a baby. The scent of baby powder, the feel of snuggly blankets, the sight of someone so tiny, so helpless and so beautiful would have been her undoing. And now her father wanted her to take a baby into her home?

The side door opened and Cynthia Smith walked in carrying six-month-old Gino Andreas in a baby carrier, along with a diaper bag and a duffel.

Her father squeezed her hand again. "Your mother and I have been keeping Gino during the Andreas funerals, but it's time you took him." He rose and accepted the baby carrier from Cynthia. "Thank you, Cyn."

She nodded and her blond hair bobbed. "You're welcome, sir."

As Cynthia left the room, Whitney's father set the carrier on the sofa, pulled Gino out and presented the dark-haired, dark-eyed baby boy to her. "He's yours, Whitney."

Knowing there was no arguing with her father, Whitney slid the envelope into her jacket pocket and took the six-month-old with shaking hands. He immediately began to cry.

"Don't cry, sweetie," she crooned, automatically pressing his head to her shoulder to comfort him. "It's okay."

Her instinctive response to his crying amazed her, but she wasn't surprised by the pain that sliced through her—the memories that flashed through her brain. Her daughter had been a tiny blonde with huge blue eyes. She'd rarely cried, except when she missed her mother. She'd loved bananas and puppies. To Whitney, she'd seemed the smartest baby on the face of the earth.

Tears filled her eyes. Her stomach tightened. She couldn't do this.

Maybe she needed more time with her therapist, Dr. Miller?

But before she could say anything to her dad, the office door opened. Wearing jeans, cowboy boots and a cable-knit sweater, Cade Andreas entered first. Behind him was Nick, the dark-haired, dark-eyed brother who most resembled the senior Andreas. And finally

Darius. Taller than their father, but with eyes and hair as dark as his, striking in his expensive business suit, Darius was very clearly the leader of the group.

Their expressions were solemn, yet strong. Almost arrogant. The head of the Andreas family was dead. They now controlled one of the largest shipping conglomerates in the world.

Or so they thought.

She glanced at the baby in her arms. For the first time in three years she felt a swell of protectiveness only a mother could feel, and she understood why Missy had given *her* custody along with Darius. The Andreas men were strong. Maybe too strong. And babies needed love.

The question was did she have any left to give?

"Are you kidding me?"

Darius Andreas gaped at Gerard Ross, his deceased father's attorney, then at Gerard's daughter Whitney Ross, a tall, cool blonde with gray-blue eyes who looked nothing like her short, round father. The pair sat on the black leather sofa. The Andreas brothers sat across from them on three black leather chairs. Beside Whitney was a baby carrier and inside the carrier was a baby boy who looked to be only a few months old. His black hair and dark eyes marked him as an Andreas as clearly as Gerard Ross's pronouncement did.

"I assure you, there's no joke." Gerard leaned back, getting more comfortable. "This little boy is your father's final son. There are four of you now."

He picked up the will and began reading again. "It is my wish that the remaining two-thirds share of Andreas Holdings be divided equally among my four sons—Darius, Cade, Nick and Gino."

Gino.

A baby.

His final half-sibling was a baby!

Darius sucked in a breath, forcing that to sink in, but it wouldn't. His brain had frozen. He was stunned, speechless and working not to lose his temper over something he couldn't change. Nick and Cade appeared to be equally shell shocked.

Finally, the business sense Darius had trusted his entire life came to his rescue. "I want a DNA test."

The smooth leather sofa sighed when Gerard sat forward. He looked down at his entwined fingers, then caught Darius's gaze.

"Your father might not have married Missy Harrington, but he's named on the birth certificate as Gino's father. Had Missy not died with your father, you might be fighting her for the company right now."

"I still want DNA."

"I understand you're surprised—"

"Surprised? How about shocked? First our father calls us to the hospital after the accident to tell us that he gave one-third interest in the company to someone else. So we'll never fully own our own damned company. Then he tells us *we* have no sense of family and unless we pull together we're going to lose everything he built. Then he dies. Just like that." He snapped his fingers. "Now you're telling us there's a fourth brother?"

"Mr. Andreas, the very fact that you didn't know your father had another child is proof that your sense of family leaves a bit to be desired."

Darius nearly cursed. Who was his womanizing father to tell him that he had no sense of family? His father had abandoned his mother. Hell, Stephone had abandoned *him* until he was in his teens. And then he'd appeared in Darius's life only because he had wanted to ensure that Darius went to a good university so he could be groomed to work for Andreas Holdings.

"For decades our father preached that we shouldn't take family troubles to outsiders." He rose. "Yet it looks like that's exactly what he's done." He reached for the baby carrier. Now that the shock was receding, things were beginning to sink in and make sense. He didn't really need DNA to tell him this was his brother. His father had been living with a thirty-year-old woman. It was no shock she'd gotten pregnant. Gino had all the physical markings of an Andreas. With his father's name on the birth certificate and Gino's name in the will, this little boy was family. And his father wanted him to care for him. So he would. Unlike his two brothers, Darius had always done what their father had asked.

"We'll take our brother and go now."

Whitney held back the carrier. "Dad?"

Gerard said, "There's more."

Darius just barely controlled his rising fury. *"More?"*

"You, Darius, get custody of Gino, but you share it with Whitney."

He turned his heated gaze on her.

Her yellow hair was probably pretty, but she had it rolled in a tight, no-nonsense bun at the back of her head. Her gray suit hid any hint of the body beneath it. He caught the gaze of her blue-gray eyes. In spite of the fact that she dressed to downplay her appearance, Darius felt a click of attraction. And it was mutual. He saw the flicker in her pretty blue orbs.

"It's up to you how you divide Gino's time. If you want to have him three days a week and Whitney four, or if you want to have him for two weeks a month and Whitney two, whatever you choose is up to you two. But she will vote his share at your board of directors meetings."

This time Darius did curse. But he quickly pulled in a breath, struggling to rein in his temper, and glanced again at Whitney. The click of attraction he'd felt when he'd first looked into her eyes turned into a current of electricity that zapped between them. They were definitely attracted.

If this were any other day, any other time, any other circumstance, he would have pursued her. Peel off a few layers of clothes, take down her hair—he was just about certain he'd find paradise.

But those eyes, those pretty Persian-cat eyes, told him to forget it. It didn't matter if they were attracted to each other. They had a job to do. Raise Gino. Together.

* * *

Whitney stayed perfectly still under Darius Andreas's scrutiny, though warm, sweet attraction hummed through her. She ignored it. He was a gorgeous man with his dark, brooding good looks, his tailored suit made to accentuate his broad shoulders and trim hips, and his commanding personality. Any woman would react to him. Simply from the way his other brothers hadn't even spoken since introductions were made, it was clear that Darius was the brother in charge. And that was very sexy.

With his piercing onyx eyes boring into hers, she suppressed a shiver. But she wasn't worried about falling victim to the attraction. Attractions frequently grew into relationships and relationships made people vulnerable. The pain that had followed the loss of her husband had been indescribable. She'd never put herself through that again. She'd never even let herself get close. She couldn't be attracted to Darius Andreas. She refused.

Darius squeezed his eyes shut in disgust and popped them open again. "All right. Fine." He motioned for Whitney to follow him. "Let's go."

"Go?"

"If this baby's on the board, he's working for a living."

Whitney's dad laughed. "Very funny, Darius."

"I'm not laughing. My father left the company in a sad state. There's work to do. And nobody's excused. Since your daughter has his vote, she'll pull his share of the duty."

"That's preposterous—"

"Dad." Whitney interrupted her father. "It's okay. I've never been one to shirk my responsibilities." She straightened her shoulders and looked Darius in the eye, accepting his challenge. If he thought he'd intimidate her on day one, he was sadly mistaken. She could handle a little work. "If everybody's working, then I will, too."

"All right," her dad agreed, "but before anybody leaves there's one more thing."

Darius turned. His dark eyes were ablaze now.

Whitney's dad looked from Darius to Cade to Nick and back at Darius again. "With someone else in possession of a one-third share of Andreas Holdings, and four brothers sharing the other two-thirds, you don't have to be a math scholar to know that individually none of you has controlling interest in the whole company." He glanced from Darius to Cade to Nick again. "Your father has instructed me to allow the holder of the one-third interest to remain anonymous until she decides how to handle her position. She's in her seventies, so she may simply want to sit back and enjoy the profits. But if she decides she wants to be active in the company, you had better be united or Andreas Holdings will end up being run by somebody other than an Andreas."

"We'll need a few minutes." Past being shocked by the conditions and warnings coming out of his dad's lawyer's mouth, Darius spoke quietly, with the authority of command. "We'd appreciate the use of your office to discuss this."

Gerard Ross rose. "Whitney and I will take Gino to her office. Have Cynthia call us when you're ready."

Gerard and Whitney left the room through a side door and Darius faced his brothers. "This wasn't exactly how we expected the reading of the will to turn out."

Nick snorted a laugh, but Cade rose. "Frankly, with the exception of Gino, nothing that happened this morning surprised me. You got most of the goodies, Darius. The Montauk estate and the chairmanship, but I think it all evens out with you also getting the baby." He saluted and headed for the door. "Good luck with that."

Right. Cade. The rebel. He should have

guessed he wouldn't hang around to lend a helping hand and probably neither would Nick. There was no love, loyalty or unity among the Andreas brothers. They'd gone their separate ways, managed their trust funds individually, made their own fortunes. And each of them had his own life. But after Attorney Ross's warning about the mystery shareholder, Darius was beginning to understand some of the things their father had babbled about on his deathbed. If they weren't unified when that shareholder came out of the woodwork they could end up dockworkers in their own shipyards.

"Come on. You can't just walk away." He motioned for Cade to return to his seat, but instead, Nick rose.

"Sure we can. You're the chairman and CEO. You're the one who has to run things. You might have bullied Ms. Ross into working for you, but we're not buying in. We'll be back for board of directors meetings and for our share of the profits."

"So you really are just going to leave? Even after Dad told us he wanted us to unite? Even after hearing there's another shareholder?"

"You'll handle it."

"This company belongs to *all* of us. I thought you'd both want a part of things."

"Yeah, and I thought Dad would be around when I was a kid. But he wasn't." Nick caught Darius's gaze. "You were the golden boy. The company, the baby, the troubles are all yours."

He left the room with Cade right behind him.

Darius fell to the sofa. Over the years he'd cursed his dad for being a philanderer who had created three very different sons…four now. Today he looked up at the ceiling, finally understanding what had troubled his father for the last ten years of his life. The Andreas brothers truly weren't family. Having three different moms and hailing from three different parts of the United States, they were as divided as they were different. They might share dark hair, dark eyes and a shrewd business sense, but there was no love lost between them.

The silence of the lawyer's office rattled around him. Both of his parents were dead now. He had no cousins or aunts and uncles. He had two adult half-brothers, but they wanted nothing to do with him.

He thought back a few weeks to Christmas. He'd gone to parties galore, but on Christmas morning he'd been alone. His footsteps had echoed in his cold, empty apartment. Unless he did a better job of raising Gino than his father had done with him, Nick and Cade, this would be the sound of his life. Silence.

In a weird way, he was glad he'd gotten custody of Gino. Gino was his family now.

Well, his and Whitney Ross's.

A sliver of excitement slithered through him when he remembered the feeling of attraction that had arced between him and Whitney. Oh, she was tempting. A challenge. A buttoned-down present, begging to be unwrapped. But that would be nothing but trouble. He had to raise a child with her.

He understood why Missy Harrington had recognized that Gino would need a mother figure. Anybody who spent two minutes in the company of any of the Andreas brothers knew they weren't the settling-down kind. So if Missy wanted a mother for Gino, she'd probably known she'd have to pick her. But he didn't have a clue how "shared custody" would work in the real world. Would sharing a child be like being married? Or maybe being divorced? Would they have to draw up a custody agreement that set forth who got the baby and when? Or would they pass the poor kid back and forth like a tennis ball or Frisbee?

He ran his hands down his face. He had

absolutely no idea how this would go. Worse, he had no idea how to care for a baby. Hell, he just plain had no idea how to be a dad, since his own father hadn't come around until he was nearly an adult.

Which gave Whitney a second, maybe more important, role in this child-custody venture. Because Darius didn't know how a father was supposed to behave, Whitney was going to have to teach him.

CHAPTER TWO

As WHITNEY AND HER DAD left his office, Cyn caught his arm. "They need you in the conference room right now."

"But I'm still working with the Andreas brothers—"

"The exact words Roger said were, 'The Mahoney case is going to hell in a ham sandwich. The very second Gerry is out of his meeting we need him in here.'"

Whitney's dad faced her. "Will you be okay?"

She forced a smile. "Yes. You go on. When the Andreas brothers are through with their little powwow, I'll have you paged if we need you."

"Thanks." He kissed her cheek, slid the duffel and diaper bag onto her shoulder, turned and raced away from her.

Walking to her office, Whitney looked down at Gino. Sucking a green-and-brown camouflage-print pacifier, he peered up at her. Luminous dark eyes met hers. Her heart stumbled in her chest. Layla's pale-blue eyes had been a combination of her father's sky blue eyes and Whitney's gray blue. Her hair had been yellow. Baby-fine. Wispy. Whitney had never been able to get a clip to hold and she'd become one of those moms who used multicolored cloth hair bands to decorate her baby's head.

Her chest tightened. She'd give everything she had, everything she owned, every day of the rest of her life, for even one more chance to touch that wispy hair.

Gino spat out his pacifier and began to cry. Whitney set the baby carrier on the small floral-print sofa in the right-hand corner of her office.

"Don't cry, sweetie," she said automatically and her throat closed. Her chest tightened. Caring for a baby was something like riding a bike. Unfortunately, all the remembered skills also brought back memories of the baby she'd lost—

The nights she'd walked the floor when Layla was colicky. Her first birthday party when the abundance of guests had scared her. Bathing her, cuddling her, loving her.

Being her mom.

Don't cry, sweetie.

She squeezed her eyes shut, trying to pull herself together, but Gino cried all the harder.

She sat on the sofa, lifted him from the carrier and cuddled him against her chest. Sobbing in earnest now, the little boy buried his face in her neck.

He smelled like baby lotion and felt as soft as feathers from an angel's wings. She closed her eyes again, weakened by longings for her own baby. Remembering treasured events. The plans they'd had for Layla's future. The mom she'd wanted to be.

Shaking with sorrow, she pushed at those memories, trying to get them out of her head. But they wouldn't budge. Instead, they arched in her brain like a rainbow of photos, a cacophony of happy sounds. Baby giggles. Toddler laughs. First words. Mama. Da Da. Nanna. Pap Pap. Kitty.

She knew it was the sweet baby scents that caused her total recall. So she grabbed a blanket from the diaper bag and laid it on the sofa, then placed Gino on top, putting three feet of distance between them.

She swallowed. The memories receded. Her shaking subsided. The thumping of her heart slowed.

The little boy blinked at her.

"I know you're probably scared," she said, talking to him as if he were an adult because she couldn't risk the baby talk that she knew would soothe him. "I know my mom was very good to you the past few days, but I'll bet you miss your own mama…" She swallowed. Miss didn't even halfway describe the feelings of loss this baby must feel. Even though he probably didn't understand that his parents were dead, *her* heart broke because she *did* understand. She knew exactly what it felt like to lose the two people closest to her. He was alone. Scared. And wanted his mom. Or someone to make him feel safe again.

In three long years, she hadn't felt safe. Everything she believed had been tossed in the air and come down in pieces the day her husband had committed suicide and killed their baby with him.

As she checked Gino's diaper to see if that was why he was crying, a rush of memories of Layla flooded her brain again. Except this time they weren't happy. This time, she heard her baby crying, calling for her, and suddenly she was face to face with her worst fear. The fear that morphed into guilt. The guilt her therapist had told her was pointless.

No one knew if Burn had deliberately put

Layla into the car with him when he'd decided to kill himself by sitting in the vehicle while the garage filled with carbon monoxide. Speculation was that he'd put Layla into her car seat to go somewhere, but when he'd gotten behind the wheel he just couldn't force himself out into the world. He'd sat in their garage long enough for the fumes to begin to get to him and was soon mentally too far gone to remember he had the baby with him.

That explanation had soothed everyone but Whitney. If everyone accepted that Burn's depression and mounting mental illness were reason enough to forget he had their child in his car, then shouldn't she have realized he was too sick to care for her baby?

Layla.

Why hadn't she recognized Burn's growing troubles?

Why hadn't she protected her baby?

What had been so important in those months that she'd missed all the signs that Burn was tumbling over the edge?

Tears filled her eyes as Gino began to cry, drawing her back to the present. She wanted to cuddle him, to love him, but her memories of Layla were still morphing into memories of Burn's suicide, Layla's death and the horrible, horrible feelings of guilt.

She couldn't deal with the guilt.

She changed Gino's diaper but rather than hold him, she returned him to the baby carrier. He looked at her with sad dark eyes.

She blinked back tears, hoping for his sake that the trouble she had holding him was only temporary. It wasn't his fault her family had died. Plus, Missy had wanted her to care for this little guy—

Remembering the envelope her dad had given her, she rose from the sofa to retrieve it from her jacket pocket. After fumbling with the seal, she pulled out the slim sheet of white stationery. Pacing in front of her sofa, she read…

Whitney…

It's funny to be writing this because I don't think you'll ever read it. Actually, I hope you never do read it. But we're having wills drawn up today and we have a baby. Plans have to be made for who will care for Gino just in case something happens. Stephone said he wanted Darius to have custody, but I didn't think that was such a good idea. I know Darius will never marry and that means Gino will never have a mom. But I also recognized I couldn't talk Stephone out of naming Darius as guardian. All I could do was suggest making you co-guardian. So that's what we did. If something happens to me and Stephone, Darius will be Gino's dad and you will be Gino's mom.

Love him, Whitney. I'm not sure Darius knows how. Missy

Whitney swallowed and sank to the couch. The note was short and to the point. A mother's simple plea. Love her baby. Because she wasn't sure his older brother knew how to love. Hadn't she already guessed that?

She glanced at Gino. The baby blinked at her dubiously. This little boy had gone from his parents' home in Greece to Whitney's parents' home, and now he was being passed to her. It had undoubtedly frightened Gino to be passed from one set of strangers to the next. He had to get into a stable environment. *She* had to get him into a stable environment. Without her, there was no guarantee Gino wouldn't be raised by nannies or at boarding school. Worse, there was no one to prevent Darius from seeing Gino more as a vote at a director's meetings than as a baby.

She had to do this. She had to be a part of

this little boy's life. She had to care for him. She had to *love* him.

She popped the pacifier into Gino's mouth again. "This has been a rough couple of days for you. But you're safe now. I'm going to take good care of you."

An arrow sliced into her heart. How could she promise she'd take good care of this little boy when she hadn't even been able to protect her own child from her husband...the baby's father?

Darius gave himself another minute to collect himself, then stepped into the hall and instructed the receptionist to let Attorney Ross know he was ready.

Pacing the rich red Oriental rug, he waited for Ross to return. When the side door opened, he spun toward it to see only Whitney enter. She held Gino in the basket-like carrier. A big duffel bag and a diaper bag were slung over her shoulder.

"I know I said I could begin working for you today, but I just realized there's no one to care for Gino. Plus, I have no baby things at my home," she announced casually as she stepped inside. "No crib, no high chair, no swing or rocker."

Darius's male senses perked up. Probably

because he and Whitney were alone for the first time. He caught the scent of her perfume on the air, noticed her legs were long and shapely.

"I was thinking I should probably make arrangements to get all of that shipped to my apartment."

Darius almost said, "Sure," if only because his immediate reaction was to give her anything she wanted. But that was his attraction talking, agreeing so she'd like him. He had to resist that. He wanted this little boy in his life. He also needed Whitney to teach him how to be a father. The only way he could see that working out would be for her and the baby to live with him—at least for the first few weeks.

"I've been thinking about this deal and I'm not sure either one or the other of us taking him is the right thing to do."

She blinked at him. "You want to leave him at a hotel?"

He chuckled, hoping she was joking. Surely she couldn't think he was that inept. "No. I'm saying we need a plan."

"We'll hammer out an agreement of some sort eventually. But he needs somewhere to stay tonight. It's already close to five and neither one of us owns a crib. We should also hire a nanny." She caught his gaze. "Unless you've got baby experience I don't know about."

Heat whipped through him. This attraction wasn't going to be easy to ignore. But he was a very strong man. "Actually, I'm going to need a little help getting accustomed to him."

She turned away, fiddled with something in the diaper bag. "We both will in the beginning."

Rats. She wasn't getting what he was driving at. He didn't want her to know just how baby-stupid he was, and he couldn't tell her without putting himself at a disadvantage. He wasn't accustomed to negotiating from anything less than a position of strength. But sometimes the best way to win an argument was to use the element of surprise. Just come right out and propose the ridiculous.

"Or we could live together."

She spun to face him. "What?"

"Look, I inherited my father's estate on Montauk. There's a house big enough that we wouldn't even have to run into each other. This way we'd both see the baby every day and we could discuss any issue that came up the minute it came up."

She didn't say anything. Darius wasn't sure if he'd taken her so much by surprise that she was speechless or if his suggestion was so ridiculous she didn't know how to respond. So he pushed on.

"It doesn't have to be forever. Only the first few weeks. That way the little guy wouldn't be shuffled from one of us to the other before he got to know either of us. Plus, we'd have servants. We wouldn't be doing this on our own."

Whitney surprised him by saying, "How many servants?"

He shrugged. "Well, if I remember correctly there are several maids. My dad also always had a cook. And an estate manager, Mrs. Tucker."

Her expression went from strained to thoughtful to sort of happily surprised. Victory surged through him. But she hadn't actually consented. The battle wasn't over yet. He needed a deal sealer. Something that would put her totally on his side.

On impulse, he walked over to her and glanced down at the baby carrier. The brown-eyed boy blinked up at him over his pacifier.

"He's cute."

"He's very cute." She paused for a heartbeat then said, "Do you want to hold him?"

"Yeah. That'd be great." How hard could it be? Not only was he trying to get on Whitney's good side, but he had to be a dad to this kid. There was no time like the present to begin learning how.

She set the carrier on her father's black leather sofa, unbuckled the strap that held Gino in and lifted him in front of her. Eye-to-eye with the baby, she said, "Gino, I'm giving you to your big brother."

Darius laughed. "Was that an introduction?"

"No. That was me preparing him to be taken by a stranger."

"He'll know?"

Her gaze met his over the baby's dark head. "Of course, he'll know."

Her eyes were the most wonderful color of gray-blue. A sort of sexy, yet innocent shade that sparked his attraction to life again. Something sharp and sweet stabbed him in his middle. He was wishing that he didn't need her so he could follow this compelling urge he had to pursue her, when she presented Gino to him and fear immediately knocked every other thought out of his brain.

But before he had a chance to panic over his first-ever attempt at holding a baby, his hand brushed Whitney's as she gave him the baby and pinpricks of awareness lit up his skin. He'd never felt an attraction this strong, this gripping. A warning stirred in his brain, but Whitney let go and suddenly Darius was supporting Gino's full weight.

"Whoa!" He bobbled him a bit before he got control. "He's heavier than I thought."

Whitney smiled slightly. "Yes. Most six-month-olds aren't quite that...sturdy."

Feeling painfully awkward, but determined to get the hang of this, Darius laughed uncomfortably. "We are a family of big eaters."

She looked away.

Not sure if she was totally disinterested in him and his family or uncomfortable at being so close to him, Darius casually said, "How about if we swing by your apartment and gather some things so we can spend the weekend in Montauk? My dad and Missy might have only popped by the house for a few weeks a year, but after Gino was born they had to have created a nursery. So at least he'll have somewhere to sleep tonight. That way you can take a look around the place and see that I'm right. The house is big enough that we could live together for a few weeks without getting in each other's way."

Whitney's skin pricked with fear, trepidation and possibility. She couldn't picture herself alone with Gino tonight. Well, actually, she could. She saw herself paralyzed with grief as he lay in the crib sobbing. Darius's suggestion that they spend the weekend together would have been the answer to a prayer, except he wouldn't be any better with Gino than she was.

Of course, he had staff and eventually they'd hire a nanny.

Still, it could take weeks to hire someone. Especially since they had to find someone willing to go back and forth between her Soho loft and Darius's estate. If they didn't have a nanny tonight, there would be no hiding the fact that she was having trouble being around the little boy. Trouble holding him. Trouble smelling him. Trouble just being in the same room.

Of course, if she had a breakdown in front of Darius it might be bad for her, but it would be good for Gino, because at least there'd be someone to pick up the ball. No matter how inexperienced. With a few quick baby lessons she could probably turn Darius into a moderately competent caregiver.

As if to confirm that idea, Darius jiggled Gino on his arm, as he cooed and gooed at him, and Gino playfully slapped his face. They liked each other. They almost appeared to have some kind of natural family bond.

Blessed relief swelled through her. It wasn't

a perfect idea, but it was better than her being alone with Gino. In the name of teaching Darius how to do his part for the little boy, she could hand over most of the tasks that might cause her to burst into tears.

Plus he had staff. Gino would be surrounded by people who could care for him until they found a nanny. And if Whitney played it right, she wouldn't even have to have a panic attack to get assistance. Gino was so adorable, every maid, cook and butler would want a turn at holding him, feeding him, rocking him to sleep.

She sucked in a breath, caught Darius's gaze, and said, "Okay. We'll spend the weekend at your house."

He smiled at her, reminding her of the other teeny, tiny thing she'd forgotten to add into the equation. They were attracted. And about to live together.

Luckily, his house was huge. And she wasn't stupid. She'd keep a cool head and everything would be fine.

CHAPTER THREE

ON THE DRIVE OUT TO Montauk, Darius called ahead to let the staff know they would be arriving.

Clicking off his call, he faced Whitney. "There's a nursery."

"Really? That's great."

"Yes. My father and Missy had been staying at the house when they were in the accident."

Sadness tiptoed through her at the loss of her friend, but she focused on the job she had to do for Missy. "So there wouldn't happen to be a nanny?"

"No. Their nanny was a young woman from Greece. She went home immediately after the funerals."

"Too bad."

He shrugged. "Not really. I'm sure we can easily hire someone."

Whitney smiled noncommittally, then her

gaze fell to Gino who was asleep in his car seat. She should have started Darius's baby lessons the minute they got into the limo. She knew what to do and his hands could be the hands that carried out her instructions tonight. But now Gino was asleep and probably wouldn't awaken until they arrived. And when he awakened, he'd be crying. Then Darius would see her struggle and fumble.

Sucking in a soft breath, she told herself not to borrow trouble. Everything would work out if she just kept a cool head.

The limo pulled up to an iron gate and the driver used a combination on a keypad to open it. As they drove up the wide, circular drive to get to the enormous house, Whitney's heart kicked into overdrive. With bare tree branches blowing in the January breeze the estate had a cold, deserted feel to it. An ominous mood that almost made her shiver. And definitely made her wonder if this was the right choice. Darius Andreas was a stranger and she'd agreed to live with him.

Whitney unbuckled Gino as the driver opened the door. He helped her out and Darius stepped out behind her, then reached inside for the baby.

Refusing to panic or let her imagination run wild over the cold, empty feeling that surrounded her, Whitney followed him to the front door, where he hit a few buttons on a hidden security panel, then opened the door.

They walked onto white marble tile in the echoing foyer. A curved stairway led the way to the second floor. A huge crystal chandelier awakened with light when Darius hit the switch as an older woman wearing a tidy black suit walked into the foyer to greet them.

"This is Mrs. Tucker," Darius said, turning to Whitney then Mrs. Tucker with a smile. "Mrs. T, this is Whitney. She's Gerard Ross's daughter."

Mrs. Tucker nodded once. "It's a pleasure to meet you, ma'am."

Whitney returned her smile. Though her parents hadn't had servants while she was growing up, and she herself had never had anything more than a cleaning service, her parents now had a full staff for their home on Park Avenue. "It's a pleasure to meet you, too, Mrs. Tucker."

"You're in the guest suite in the right wing upstairs. Geoffrey will get your bags from the limo."

"Thank you."

Mrs. Tucker turned to leave, but a thought

struck Whitney and she stopped her. "Where's the nursery?"

"In the left wing beside the master suite and Mr. Andreas."

"Will the nanny also be beside the nursery?"

"Yes, ma'am. The nanny's quarters are on one side. Mr. Andreas's are on the other."

That just didn't sit right. Not because of the unexpected jealousy that slithered through her at the thought of another woman being a door or two away from Darius's bedroom, but because she felt as if she were being eased out. She hadn't questioned Darius talking her into living at the house in Montauk. Her fears had actually caused her to be relieved he'd thought of it. But now that he'd assigned her to a room across the house from the nursery, suspicions rose in her. He wanted the baby at his house, wanted her at the other side of the mansion. What was he up to?

"Why am I not near the nursery?"

Holding Gino in the baby carrier, Darius stepped forward, caught her arm and directed her to the stairway as Mrs. Tucker scrambled away, obviously glad Darius would field the question.

"I thought you'd prefer privacy, particularly since Mrs. Tucker has agreed to sleep in the nanny's room to help with Gino until we get a regular nanny."

He sounded sincere, genuine. But this was a skilled negotiator, a smart businessman, a charming man. And her fears about caring for Gino had blinded her to the way he'd been calling the shots. That ended here. That ended now.

"Isn't there another suite close to the nursery?"

"Yes, of course."

"I'd like that one, then."

Darius stopped walking. His black onyx eyes snared hers, she was sure, in a show of strength, ready to meet her challenge. But within seconds the expression in his dark orbs shifted from serious to sensuous.

As if he only now realized how close they were standing beside each other on the stairs, he pulled in a breath. Tension rose up, shimmering through her. This man was attracted to her. There was no better aphrodisiac for a woman than the realization that a powerful, sexy man wanted her.

Her.

And she'd just insisted she be in a room closer to the nursery, *closer to him.*

She almost told him to forget about her request for a room change, but knew that if she did he'd realize it was because of their attraction. She also remembered it was her responsibility to love Gino and maybe even to protect him from overbearing Darius, and by God, she intended to. If that meant she needed to be close to him too, she'd handle it.

She smiled, hoping to appear to be a woman who hadn't even been slightly affected by the way he'd looked at her. "I take my responsibilities seriously, Darius. Though I'm glad Gino will be close to the nanny we hire, I want to be close too. The will says we share custody. I was given a job. I intend to do it."

His serious eyes suddenly filled with mischief that sent her pulse scrambling. "So you want to be across the hall—" he smiled "—from me?"

She stared into his sexy dark eyes with every nerve ending in her body humming and the blood in her veins virtually singing. Her voice squeaked when she said, "Yes."

"So be it. I'll have Mrs. Tucker tell Geoffrey to put your things in the room across the hall from mine."

With that he pulled out his cell phone, turned and walked up the stairs. Whitney nearly collapsed on the stairway. She heard him speaking on the phone, instructing someone to ready the room across the hall from his, and guessed he was talking to Mrs. Tucker. She hastily climbed the stairs with shaky legs and followed Darius to the nursery. But two steps inside the door, she froze.

A mobile over the cherrywood crib zapped her back in time. She could have been standing in Layla's nursery. The colors of the wall were different, but most of the furniture and lots of the toys were the same. So were the scents.

Darius carried the baby inside. "I think he needs a change. I'd offer to do it," he smiled engagingly, "but I've never changed a diaper in my entire life."

Smothered by thoughts of her baby, Whitney couldn't get her legs to move or her mouth to form words. Memories rolled through her mind. In perfect Technicolor she saw the vision of Layla standing up in her crib, holding the bars, crying for her mother. She remembered the Christmas gifts she had bought and hidden in the closet as if little Layla would somehow know to look for them. It had been almost a year before she had been able to clear out the nursery, if only because she couldn't step inside without crumbling.

But Darius didn't seem to notice her paralysis. Pulling Gino out of the baby carrier, he said, "I'd be happy to do it, though, if you want to teach me."

Whitney cleared her throat. "Sure." Relief swamped her. For as much as she didn't want Darius taking over Gino's life, with her grief perilously close to the surface she simply couldn't handle touching Gino right now. Whether she liked it or not, take-charge Darius was saving her.

She glanced around until she saw the changing table. She pointed at it. "Take him over there."

Darius carried the sleepy baby to the changing table.

Whitney frowned. "We left the diaper bag in the car."

"Geoffrey will get it. But there should already be diapers here somewhere. I told the staff to make sure the nursery was stocked." With one hand holding Gino in place on the table, he opened the doors of the cupboard beneath it. "Ah. There they are." He reached in and pulled one out with a smile. "The staff is very efficient."

She took a cautious step to the changing table. "So I see."

"Now what?"

Forcing back the memories, she pulled in a slow, cleansing breath. Her grief subsiding, she strolled closer. "Unsnap his pajamas and slide him out."

He unsnapped the one-piece pajamas but was a little rough in getting Gino's arm out. She laid her hand on top of his. "Gentler."

"Okay." He peeked over at her and smiled stupidly. "His skin is soft, like velvet."

She remembered thinking that very thing the first time she held Layla and swallowed back the grief, pushed back the memory of the nurse laying her brand-new baby girl into her arms. "I know."

When Gino was out of his pajamas and wearing only his diaper, Whitney pointed at the tabs of his diaper and said, "Yank on those to open the diaper."

He yanked on the tabs and to everyone's joy, the diaper was only wet.

Darius said, "Whew."

Whitney couldn't help it. She laughed. "Okay, toss that in the container beside the changing table." She motioned to the available diaper pail. "Slide another diaper under him, fasten the tabs, put him into clean pajamas and you're done."

Darius followed her instructions, needing another reminder about being gentle with Gino's little arms and legs as he tucked them into pajamas. But again he only smiled when she told him.

Her suspicions about Darius came tumbling back. He was too nice. Too eager. Once again she wondered if he wasn't trying to edge her out. "I'm surprised you want to learn all this."

He caught her gaze. "Gino is my family now."

"Oh. So you're really getting into the daddy thing?" Her voice dripped with skepticism as she asked the question, but she couldn't help it. A single man—a single *rich* man—who wanted to care for a baby was more than an anomaly. It was downright weird.

"My dad didn't have a lot of time for me." He peered over at her. "Or my brothers, and I don't want that to happen to Gino. If I'm to be his male influence, I want to do my end of the duties."

"So you're going to learn how to do *everything?*"

To her surprise, he wasn't insulted. He laughed. "Hey, I just changed a diaper. I think my commitment has been proven."

Not even close. Particularly since she didn't understand why he was making such a hands-on commitment. Sure, he didn't want Gino to grow up without a dad. She got it. But there was more here. Her lawyer's instincts had gone from suspicious to downright positive there was something here she was missing.

"Okay, then tomorrow morning, we'll hit the ground running with your baby lessons."

He laughed, but Whitney wasn't kidding. Not just because she was afraid to touch Gino too much, but because she wanted to push Darius to the wall, give him so much baby time he would own up to what was really going on.

When the baby was dressed, Darius pulled him off the table and gave him a quick hug and kissed his cheek. "Good night, little guy."

Then he handed the baby to Whitney. Preoccupied with his motives, she didn't realize what he was about to do and had to scramble to catch Gino.

But the second the yawning baby was in her arms, the feel of his ultra-soft pajamas and smooth skin kicked her back in time again. Especially, when she brought Gino to her and hugged him. The second the little boy was snuggled against her, sadness overwhelmed her. The hollow, empty feeling of loss. Echoes of Layla's giggles rolled through her brain. Memories of her lifeless body haunted her.

She pulled Gino away from her shoulder

and swallowed. Then, for Darius's benefit, she offered the baby a wobbly smile. "Good night, Gino," she whispered hoarsely, hoping Darius didn't notice she was trembling.

Because she wanted to cry. She missed her baby. She yearned for the life she'd lost. Was that so bad? So hard to understand?

She stopped. No. That wasn't so bad. Or so difficult to comprehend. In fact, the smart way to handle her situation with Gino might be to *tell* Darius about Layla and Burn. She didn't want his sympathy, but it was clear now that she would have difficulty getting adjusted to caring for a baby. Soon Darius would notice. It would be better to get the story out in the open and solicit his help than to have him see her stumble and question her ability to care for his little brother.

But tonight wasn't the night for that conversation. With his motives now in question, she knew she had to wait a bit, see what he was up to before she bared her soul. If he was trying to get the baby away from her, she didn't want to hand him over on a silver platter. She'd wait. See if he didn't tip his hand or, alternatively, convince her that his motives were good.

Once the baby was in bed, Darius caught Whitney's arm and turned her to the door.

"It's late. I'll show you to your room then we can have dinner."

Exhausted, confused and aching for privacy, she woodenly said, "I'm too tired for dinner."

"Really?" As they stepped out of the nursery and into the hall, he closed the door behind them. "I instructed Mrs. Tucker to have the cook make chicken and dumplings."

She turned, startled. "Chicken and dumplings?"

He smiled. "Yes."

How could he know her favorite food?

"I called your dad while you were in your apartment packing for the weekend." he said, undoubtedly answering the expression of confusion on her face, and directed her to walk to a door a few feet down the hall. "I figured if you could be kind enough to let me have at least the weekend with the three of us at my home, I could be gentleman enough to assure you ate well."

She quickened her steps down the hall, wishing he hadn't done something so nice when she was so tired, but at least slightly more comfortable with him. "I'll have some for lunch tomorrow."

She wasn't sure why she expected him to

argue, but her suspicions were allayed even more when he simply said, "Good enough."

He stopped at a door only a few feet from the nursery. "Your suite?"

Feeling a tad foolish, she retraced her steps and stopped in front of him. He smiled slightly. Sexily.

Strange schoolgirl nervousness swept through her, reminding her of the first time she'd ever stood by a door with a boy, knowing he was about to kiss her goodnight. Awareness tingled through her bloodstream. Her breathing went shallow and her legs turned to rubber. It had been so long since she'd reacted to a man that she'd forgotten the wonderful discomfort.

But Darius caught the doorknob and twisted it, opening the door, revealing a soft green-and-yellow room to her. Beyond the sitting room furnished with a sage-colored sofa and chair, accented by a cherrywood armoire with matching cherrywood end tables, was an open door leading to a bedroom. She could see patches of a yellow-and-sage-green bedspread. See the closed yellow drapes.

Her heart skipped a beat. The suite was calm, soothing. So different from her cool aqua and brown bedroom in her condo that she felt as if she was entering another world.

"Is something wrong?"

She spun to face him. "No. It's—" Warm, inviting, comforting. She swallowed. "—Lovely. I'm sure I'll be fine here."

"Let me make sure everything really is ready before I leave you." He stepped inside the sitting room, casually looking from left to right as he made his way to the bedroom.

Confusion buffeted her as she followed him inside. From a cursory glance into the room, it was clear that while she and Darius had been in the nursery, Mrs. Tucker had sent the staff to ready the room. He had no reason to check their work, unless he was stalling. Or unless the staff was so new to him that he didn't trust them?

That had to be it.

When he stepped inside the room she'd be sleeping in, a fresh ripple of unease passed through Whitney. It felt odd, uncomfortable to have a man who'd clearly had a sexual reaction to her standing beside the bed she would sleep in. Her chest tightened. Stupid nervousness rose up in her again, reminding her that it had been a long time, maybe too long, since she'd been alone with a man.

But his gaze was casual, touching the queen-sized bed, the bare dresser, the pale sage club chairs arranged by the window for reading.

After he'd seen everything in the bedroom, his peek into the master bath caused his expression to turn puzzled, and she had no idea why. The vanity was white oak with a glass countertop. The floors were Calcutta marble slab. A separate custom-glass tile shower was utilitarian, but the oversize, extra-deep soaking tub almost caused her to sigh with joy. She could have a bath. A nice long bath to ease away the tension and grief of this long, long day. That tub would be her haven tonight.

He glanced at her then quickly away. His expression was so odd that she peeked into the bathroom again. Her gaze lit on the huge tub and suddenly her face flamed with color.

Of course, a woman saw the tub as a haven. A man saw it as a playground.

Their eyes met and the warm syrupy feeling she'd had when she'd first seen him returned. She reminded herself he was handsome. Reminded herself that being attracted to him made her normal. Even congratulated herself on finally, finally, being attracted to someone again after three long years of mourning her deceased husband. But she concluded with a reminder that she didn't want to get involved with anyone—ever. She'd never again give another person that much power over her life.

Plus, she had custody of Darius's baby brother. The little boy whose vote on his board of directors was hers. All this "attraction" could simply be Darius angling to get on her good side so she'd vote his way at directors' meetings.

Darius rubbed his hand across the back of his neck and pointed at her door. "Since you're tired and I have things to do, I'll be going."

"Oh." That surprised her. Wouldn't someone who intended to use their attraction stay? Flirt? Instead, it seemed he couldn't wait to get away.

Disappointment flooded her, which rattled her. She didn't want him to be attracted to her, but since he was, having him not act on the attraction was the second-best thing. She shouldn't be disappointed.

She forced a smile. "Okay. Great." She headed out of the bedroom too, walking with him through the sitting room.

At the door, he was even more nervous. When their gazes bumped, she knew why. They stood about a foot apart, at the door, saying goodbye. He looked down at her. She gazed up at him. Attraction shimmied between them. The urge to kiss goodbye was like a physical thing. So strong, yet so foreign, it paralyzed her.

For the first time since her husband's suicide, she wasn't thinking about her broken life. In fact, it wasn't even getting half of her attention. His nearness dominated her mind. She couldn't think beyond the fear that he'd kiss her.

Then she realized she didn't fear he'd kiss her. She *wanted* him to kiss her. What she felt was glorious, spine-tingling anticipation. Not fear.

Dear God.

Curiosity and confusion combined and rumbled through her. How could she possibly be so attracted to Darius Andreas that she couldn't ignore it? That she wanted more.

But he didn't kiss her. He didn't even try. Instead he grabbed the doorknob at the same time that she did and their fingers brushed. Though she jerked away, the mere touch sent a maelstrom through her. It had been three long years since she'd been married, and for months before that her husband hadn't been interested in her. She hadn't been touched by a man she found attractive in nearly four years. Sensation after sensation poured through her, almost embarrassing in their intensity.

Darius quickly headed out the door. "I'll see you at breakfast tomorrow."

The door closed behind him before she could even answer. Knowing it was coming, she quashed her confusing disappointment when it was just a wisp, before it had a chance to fully form, because it was ridiculous. Stupid.

She shook her head. After that little episode by the door, she didn't have any doubt that Darius was attracted to her. After the way he ran, she also knew he didn't want to be.

And that was good.

Wasn't it?

She sighed with disgust at her foolish ambiguity. This weekend was not about an inappropriate attraction. It was about figuring out how they'd raise Gino together, about helping Gino grow accustomed to them as they got to know each other—

Worry gripped her. She couldn't tell Darius about losing her husband and child without making herself look like an empty, sad, still-grieving woman, who wasn't ready to help him with Gino. Though part of her knew that was true and she should be honest, the other part warned her to tread lightly with this man. He was rich, powerful. If she showed her weakness too soon, he could take her to court, seeking full custody, citing her incompetence. Then Gino would be raised by him. Alone. And she wouldn't be able to fulfill Missy's wish that she love her baby.

She couldn't let Missy's son be raised only by Darius. Hadn't he gotten her into his house and almost put her into a room on the other side of the mansion? He'd have poor Gino in boarding school before he was four.

The thought of sweet baby Gino in a boarding school shored up her defenses and she felt herself growing ready to protect him. She would fight to her last breath before she let him put that child in boarding school—ever. And that wouldn't be their only argument. She and Darius would have hundreds of fights over the course of raising his half-brother.

That thought caused her to fall to a chair in complete shock. In the confusion of the day, she hadn't carried this guardianship all the way through in her head. But it was suddenly abundantly clear that whether they wanted it or not, this child bound them forever.

They might as well be married.

Or divorced.

Good God.

What had Missy gotten her into?

Tonight was supposed to have been the night she did her laundry. Instead, here she was in the home of a virtual stranger, with a baby who made her relive the best and worst part of her life and a man she was so attracted to she sometimes couldn't breathe in his presence.

It would be a miracle if she survived the weekend, let alone a lifetime.

CHAPTER FOUR

WHEN THE BABY AWAKENED at about three, Darius bolted up in bed. For a few seconds he was disoriented, then he remembered he was in the hideous floral and lace master bedroom of the house in Montauk. By the time he remembered Gino was in the room next door, the little boy's crying had stopped.

He got out of bed anyway, grabbed one of the pairs of jeans he'd had his staff pack and messenger to the estate and jumped into them. Heading out of the closet, he opened another drawer and snagged a T-shirt.

In a few long strides, he was at the door that connected his room to the nursery. Mrs. Tucker sat in the rocker feeding Gino, who gulped noisily.

He tiptoed into the room, but Mrs. Tucker laughed. "No need to be quiet now. He's wide awake."

Leaning against the crib, Darius crossed

his arms on his chest. "And by the looks of things he's starving too."

Mrs. Tucker snorted a laugh. "They always are."

"Always? You mean this isn't an isolated incident? He's going to be getting up at three every night?"

"Maybe not on the dot, but, yes, he'll be waking somebody up in the middle of the night every night until he learns to sleep for long stretches without needing a bottle."

Staring at the dark-haired, dark-eyed little baby, Darius said only, "Hum." Gino was so sturdy that he looked packed into the green one-piece pajama. His hair sort of stuck up in all directions, making him even cuter.

Gino stopped sucking and Mrs. Tucker set the bottle on the table by the rocker. She lifted him up and he suddenly belched loudly. Mrs. Tucker laughed. "Well, now that takes care of that."

She reached for a tissue in the box also on the table beside the rocker and wiped away white gunk from Gino's mouth.

Darius winced. "Am I ever going to get the hang of this?"

"Eventually." She caught his gaze and smiled. "And just when you do the rules will change."

Darius's face fell. "What rules?"

Settling Gino on her lap to rock him, Mrs. Tucker laughed again. "Not exactly rules, but the things you'll need to do. He's a baby now. In a few months he'll be a toddler. Then there are the terrible twos—"

"Terrible twos?"

"You don't want to know about that yet."

He did but he also didn't. Because right now, falling asleep in Mrs. Tucker's arms, Gino looked like an angel. Darius swallowed. Strong, protective feelings rose up in him, feelings more intense than anything he'd ever felt.

He pushed them down. He might intend to be a part of this kid's life, but these feelings were weird. They had to be wrong.

Mrs. Tucker rose from the rocker and settled the sleeping baby in the crib. "Better go back to bed. Morning comes quickly when you have a baby."

Darius headed for the door. "Good night."

Heading for the opposite door, Mrs. Tucker whispered, "Good night."

In his room, he crawled back into bed. He didn't like the idea that Mrs. Tucker had to do double duty, as his estate manager and the temporary nanny, so he set his alarm for six, hoping he'd get up before the baby.

When it went off a few short hours later, he didn't balk or linger. He quickly pulled on the jeans from the night before and a fisherman-knit sweater and, paying no mind to his bare feet, raced to the nursery.

"Good morning."

Dressed in jeans and a pretty blue sweater that brought out the blue of her eyes, Whitney stood on the far side of the crib, watching Gino, who was still asleep.

"Do you want to learn how to feed him this morning?"

He took an instinctive step back. He and Whitney had shared a powerful few minutes at her bedroom door the night before, but she didn't appear to be any the worse for the wear. Like him, she seemed to want to ignore their chemistry.

And he did want to feed the baby. But before he could say that, Gino's eyes fluttered open. He yawned and stretched and then let out with a yelp.

"That's your cue," Whitney said with a laugh. "Change his diaper, while I get a bottle."

Whitney calmly walked to the small fridge in the room and retrieved a bottle, which she put in the warmer.

Not wanting to jeopardize the peace between

them or have Gino wake poor, sleeping Mrs. Tucker, Darius carried Gino to the changing table and simply did the things he'd done the night before when he changed the baby's diaper and put him into a clean sleeper.

Gino wasn't really happy about the arrangement and he began to scream. Darius noticed that Whitney was preoccupied with staring at a bottle warmer that seemed not to need her attention. It confused him that she didn't react to Gino's crying, but he wanted to learn how to care for this kid. He also wanted Whitney's help. He wanted them to get along, be a team. He couldn't complain about the tasks she gave him to do. He had to do them.

When the light on the warmer went out, Darius was already on the rocker, holding screaming Gino over his shoulder.

Whitney winced. "Do you still want to feed him?"

In spite of Gino's screaming, Darius casually said, "Sure. But you're going to have to tell me what to do."

"Arrange him across your lap so that his head is supported by your forearm."

Peeling crying Gino off his shoulder wasn't an easy task. He stiffened his limbs and refused to settle on Darius's lap.

Whitney handed him the bottle. "Here.

Take this. Let him see the bottle is coming and he'll calm down."

With both hands busy with the baby, Darius didn't have a clue how to take the bottle, but he secured Gino as best he could with one hand and managed to get the other free to take the bottle.

He would have criticized Whitney for not helping, except as soon as he had the bottle in his hand, Gino began to calm down.

"Now, just press the nipple to his lips and he'll do the rest."

To Darius's complete amazement, as soon as he nudged the nipple against Gino's lips he not only stopped crying, he also started suckling loudly.

He laughed with relief. "Wow. That was different."

"Babies *are* different. They can't talk so you have to understand their crying and sometimes watch their body language."

"There's a lot to learn."

As Gino greedily gobbled his milk, Whitney walked away from the rocker and paced the room. Darius watched her for a few seconds, confused. She was in the room, but detached. Not like someone who didn't want to help, but like…well, a stranger. That was when he realized she might not know Gino any more than he did.

"So why did Missy make you guardian?"

She faced him, her expression rye. "You mean aside from the fact that she wanted to make sure her baby had a female influence?"

He laughed. "Yes. Why you?"

"Missy and I were very close from university until the day she met your dad."

"Really?"

"Her dad had left her mom before Missy was six, and her mom was an alcoholic who went in and out of rehab. Because she had money enough to have a maid, somebody who by default took care of Missy, no one ever realized how alone Missy was. So after we met, she began to come to my parents' house with me on weekends and holidays." She shrugged. "We were like sisters."

"And then she met my dad and none of us saw either one of them again."

She laughed sadly. "Missy really loved your dad."

"And he loved Greece."

"And that's where they lived."

They fell silent again. When the baby was done eating, he showed Whitney the empty bottle. "Now what?"

"Now you have to burp him."

"Burp him?"

"You hold him like this," Whitney said as she lifted Gino from Darius's lap up to his shoulder. "And pat his back."

As she said the words, she demonstrated by patting the baby's back. He burped noisily.

Whitney smiled and set Gino on his lap again. "That feels better, doesn't it, little guy?"

This close, her smoky, sexy voice curled around Darius and he nearly squeezed his eyes shut. That voice would be trouble if he heard it for several weeks with her living under his roof. Even the way she'd refused dinner the night before had been breathy and sensual. And then there was that tub. And the look that had passed between them.

He bounced out of the chair. "So do we take him down to breakfast with us or what?"

"Is there a high chair by the table?"

He nodded. "Yes."

"Then I think we should keep him with us."

"Okay."

After all the time he'd already spent with the baby, Darius didn't feel uncomfortable holding Gino, but that in itself was odd. The powerful feeling he'd had the night before came back full force. Sacred, reverent, it squeezed his heart and made breathing difficult.

Since his father's death, everything had happened so fast that he hadn't had time to think anything through. But suddenly everything seemed so real. He had a child to raise, responsibilities beyond money and food. This kid would take up his time, change his morning routine, break into his afternoons, want his evenings. The understanding of what he'd taken on was so overwhelming that he felt as though he needed a minute.

He held Gino out to Whitney. "Could you hold him while I grab some shoes?"

She hesitated and Darius nearly groaned. The last thing he wanted to do was give her the impression he didn't want the task of caring for the baby. He wanted her to see his commitment.

"You know what? Never mind. I'll take him into my bedroom with me."

To his surprise, Whitney smiled. "And what will you do with him while you're putting on your shoes?"

He sucked in a breath. "Good question."

She took Gino from him. "Go get your shoes."

Relief poured through him. He raced into his bedroom, slid into socks and shoes and was back in the nursery in less than two minutes.

Noting that Gino was in the playpen, he frowned. "Ready for breakfast?"

"Yes." She reached down and lifted Gino out of the playpen, then handed him to Darius casually, smoothly, but as he took the little boy, she wouldn't look at him.

He hadn't expected her to put Gino in the playpen or to immediately pass him back when he returned from getting his shoes. But her not being able to look at him was actually more perplexing.

The night before, he'd walked away from the opportunity to kiss her without any hesitation, even though she was throwing off you-can-kiss-me signals. He'd hoped that walking away would show her that even though he was attracted to her, he didn't intend to follow through. Yet she still behaved in an overly cautious manner around him.

She strode to the door as if nothing were amiss and held it open while he came through with the baby. Following her down the steps, he stared at her stiff back. He'd never met a woman who was so hot one minute and so cold the next. It was almost as if she could turn her emotions off.

Which, in some ways, was good. They

didn't want to be attracted to each other. It didn't work for either of them. And he was turning off his feelings for her every bit as much.

So why did it bother him?

In the breakfast room, which was actually one of several sunrooms along the east wall of the house, she took the tray off the high chair and instructed Darius to set the baby on the seat.

"But don't let go," she said, rummaging along the edges of the seat until she found what looked like seatbelts. "We have to buckle him in."

"Got it," Darius said, eager to learn. Especially when she didn't even seem to realize she was giving him lessons.

Another good reason to persuade her to live here with him permanently, not just for a few weeks.

Cook entered the sunroom with coffee and asked what each would like to eat. Darius ordered pancakes. Whitney chose a bagel and cream cheese.

"And should I make the baby's cereal?"

Darius glanced over at Whitney, who winced. "Wow. It's been so long since I was around a baby that I forgot that some kids start eating cereal around six months or so."

Cook proudly said, "He's been eating cereal for a few weeks now."

"Then get us the cereal." She faced Darius. "Sorry about that."

"Hey, I didn't even know babies ate cereal."

Cook walked in with a small bowl and a tiny baby spoon. As if recognizing his bowl, the baby slapped his hands on the tray. Cook handed the bowl and spoon to Darius who set them on the table then edged his seat closer to the high chair.

He didn't even consider opting out of learning how to feed Gino. He wanted to know everything. "So you're ready for this, huh?"

Gino screeched with joy.

Whitney said, "Just put a little bit of cereal on the spoon and very easily guide it to his mouth."

Darius did as instructed. Gino greedily took the bit of cereal and smacked his lips. The second bite was a little messier, but Darius just used common sense about getting the spoon and the cereal into Gino's mouth. After a few spoonfuls, when Gino tried to blow bubbles with it instead of eating it, Darius knew he wasn't hungry anymore.

"If you're playing in it rather than eating, I'm guessing you're done."

As he set the spoon down, Mrs. Tucker

walked in. "Cook didn't want to start your breakfast until you were free to eat it. So, I thought I'd take Gino upstairs and play with him a bit. I'll walk through the kitchen to let Cook know she can make your breakfast now."

Darius rose and helped her get the baby out of the high chair. "Sounds good."

When she left, the little room fell silent.

Finally, Whitney said, "It's beautiful here."

Darius looked out at the steel-gray ocean, the deceptively blue sky. Though the day seemed calm, he knew winds off the sea would make it freezing cold out there. "Yes. I'd forgotten."

"Did you come here often?"

"After I turned eighteen I did."

"Why do I get the feeling you were forced?"

Her perceptiveness made him wince. "Because I was. My father gave me access to a five-million-dollar trust fund when I turned eighteen. He told me it was mine but he wanted me to go to college and work for Andreas Holdings. He hadn't as much as visited after he left my mom, then suddenly he was in my life, ordering me around. Our time here wasn't always pleasant."

She toyed with a salt shaker. "I liked your dad."

He laughed as Cook brought in his pancakes and Whitney's bagel. When she was gone, he reached for the maple syrup and said, "Most people who didn't have my dad for a lover or a parent did like him."

"Yes, I suppose that's probably true."

Surprised by her answer, he set the maple syrup on the table. "I thought for sure you'd sing his praises."

She snorted a laugh. "I know what it's like to deal with a person who has a public personality and a private one. I had a husband everybody loved."

His brows rose. So she'd been married? He hadn't even considered the possibility since she'd kept the last name Ross. But having been married, maybe even having been hurt by a divorce, might explain why she was so nervous around him.

Better than that, though, she'd opened the door for him to question her about her past. He'd been so focused on the baby that he hadn't really given much thought to the woman who shared custody beyond asking why Missy had chosen her.

Pretending great interest in his coffee, he said, "Everybody loved your husband but you?"

"Oh, I loved him. He loved himself too."

She reached for the cream. "So what are your plans for the day?"

He recognized a change of subject when he heard it and realized that though she'd opened the door to talk about her past, she hadn't done it deliberately. He was curious about her, but he also knew asking about a husband she no longer had was a tad intrusive. It had no bearing on their situation and was none of his business. And if he wanted to convince her he was harmless, it would be wise to follow her lead and let the subject change.

"Actually, I want to spend as much time with the baby as I can."

She set her bagel on her plate and studied him. Her narrowed eyes were both suspicious and skeptical. "So, you weren't kidding. You really want to be a good dad?"

"I want to be a *great* dad." The words rolled through him. Now that he'd spent time with Gino, they meant so much more than they had even the day before. Now, he knew the cost. He was taking responsibility for another person.

It didn't confuse him as it had the night before or overwhelm him the way it had in the nursery that morning, but he was smart enough that it still sort of scared him. Especially since he'd vowed that he wouldn't be a part-time, no-show dad the way his father had been. Deep down inside, he had to admit he wasn't entirely sure he could do that. The only role model he'd had was a poor one.

Still, that wasn't something he could confide to Whitney. Technically, she was still a stranger. So, taking his cue from her when the conversation turned to something she hadn't wanted to tell him, he also changed the subject.

"What are *your* plans for the day?"

"I'm working on a class action case with my dad. Depositions are in. He's read them. I haven't." She grimaced. "That's never happened before."

Knowing he could get Mrs. Tucker to help him with Gino that morning and eager to make Montauk a comfortable home to Whitney, he turned his attention to his pancakes. "There are three offices in this house. You can have your choice. And you can spend the whole day if you need it. Mrs. Tucker and I will take care of Gino."

Relief saturated her voice. "Thanks."

She worked all day, stopping only to have lunch around two, long after Darius and Gino had eaten so she didn't have to interact with either one of them. But she couldn't get out of dinner. She arrived in the formal dining room at seven, dressed as she had been all day in jeans and a bulky sweater.

Darius, who was already seated at the head of the table, rose.

He still wore the fisherman-knit sweater and jeans he'd put on in the morning. Holding out the chair at the place beside his, he explained, "I assumed you'd be too busy to change."

She sat. "Yes. Thank you."

"My father insisted everything be formal. I'm more accommodating." He shook out his napkin. "I hope you like Italian."

"Actually, I love most foods." She risked a glance at him and fought a quiver of attraction. That morning she'd noticed that he looked very good in the casual clothes, but tonight he hadn't shaved. The scruffy stubble on his chin and cheeks made him sexy in a disreputable, sinful way. The man was simply too handsome for his own good and she was vulnerable. She hadn't interacted with a man like this—single and attractive—since she'd met her husband. She was out of practice, attracted and needy. A deadly combination when three feet away from a gorgeous man. Especially when she didn't want to get involved with another man.

But she couldn't be a total grouch or, worse,

an unappreciative guest. "You don't have to worry when it comes to me and food. I'd eat constantly if I didn't have work to keep me busy."

He laughed. Pinpricks of delight raced up her spine. It had been so long since she'd made a man laugh in simple conversation that she'd forgotten the joy of it.

"I don't believe it." His gaze rippled down the lines of her body and lingered on her breasts. "Your figure's too nice."

Good Lord! He was flirting with her!

The desire to flirt back shoved at her. It rattled through the recesses of her brain like a prisoner banging the bars of his cell, longing for release. Especially with the joy of having just made him laugh taunting her, reminding her of what it felt like to be normal.

But it had been so long since she'd done anything even remotely like flirt, and he was absolutely the wrong guy to experiment with—

Or was he? They both needed each other too much professionally to cross any lines. He'd walked away from the perfect opportunity to kiss her the night before, proving that he might be attracted to her, but he didn't intend to follow through. And she was too frightened of relationships to let anything she attempted go any further than flirting. He might actually be the perfect person to practice on.

She smiled, trying not to look obvious, trying not to look self-conscious, trying desperately to look simply like a single woman flirting with a single man. "I'll bet you say that to all the girls."

He laughed again. "Only the really pretty ones."

Joy exploded inside her. She'd done it! Or maybe *they* were doing it. Flirting. Getting her back into the real world. What was a simple conversation for him was turning into a monumental event for her. But she hoped to God he didn't realize that.

A younger woman served dinner, standing off to the side to attend to their every need, precluding any possibility that the conversation could become intimate. The flirting stopped, but the discussion stayed casual, neutral and she relaxed totally.

At the end of the meal, Darius rose. "How about a game of pool?"

"Pool?"

"You know balls, sticks, table with green felt?"

She laughed then marveled that she had. Maybe her dad was right. Maybe it was time. She wanted so badly to be normal again. Real.

Honest. Just herself. And Darius seemed to have the power to help her take the steps.

Still, no good would come of pushing things.

"I don't think so, I'm—"

"Tired? Really, Ms. Ross? I'm about to suggest you take some vitamins."

She laughed again, feeling light, young, incredibly carefree. Memories of her other life, her sadness, nudged at her, but she shoved them back. She needed this. She *wanted* this.

He directed her to the door on the right. "Come on. This house is filled with things to entertain us. It would be a shame not to take advantage. Particularly since we're going to be spending lots of time together over the next eighteen years. We should get to know each other."

Fear and elation collided, creating goose bumps on her upper arms. Getting to know each other didn't have to be something to be afraid of or even something sexual. He wanted the same thing she did. Nothing sinister. Nothing difficult. Just a simple evening spending time together. To get to know each other. Because they had joint custody of a child.

Inclining her head in acceptance, she ignored

the fear and tamped down the elation and reminded herself that spending time getting to
know each other didn't have to be a big deal.
She didn't have to tell him about her family
that night. She could wait for a more suitable
time. Tonight, he was only asking for a game
of pool.

"All right."

The room with the pool table was a huge
den. Cherrywood walls and leather furniture
gave the space a totally masculine feel.

"Your dad's room, I assume," she said,
walking to a wall lined with sticks, as Darius
gathered and racked the balls.

"Got it in one." He ambled over to choose a
stick. "But before you begin feeling sorry for
Missy, take a look around. They might have
lived in Greece, but they spent time here. Her
influence is all over the place."

"Really?"

"She's redone at least three rooms." He
winced. "Including the master bedroom."

"You don't like her taste?"

"If you're asking if I like floral bedspreads
and lacy curtains, then no."

She laughed, glad she'd agreed to spend
some time with him. Over the next half hour
they played several games of pool and he
handily beat her.

"You're a ringer."

"Ringers make you believe they're terrible so they can persuade you to bet them, and then they take your money. I haven't done that." He shrugged. "We're just having a nice friendly few games."

"With me getting my butt beaten."

He racked the balls and broke, scattering the colorful orbs across the table with a clack and clatter. In an uncharacteristic turn of events, none of them fell into a pocket.

"Hey! Looks like I get a turn this time."

She walked around the table, sizing up potential shots. When she found one she liked, she angled her stick across the table, levering her body in sync with the stick.

"No. No. You'll never make the shot that way." He strode around the table to her. "Let me help you." He lowered himself over her, his one hand covering hers on the stick, his other circling around her so he could guide her hand on the handle.

Her nerve endings exploded at the contact. Rivers of molten need rode her blood. And she remembered why they had to be careful. Even about becoming friends. Their attraction was like nitroglycerin. One bump and they could go up in flames.

As if realizing how close he'd put them, he

turned his head and caught her gaze. Their faces were only millimeters apart. His warm breath fanned her face. Longing burst inside her. Her fingers itched to touch the stubble on his cheeks and cruise his throat. Just a brush. Just a touch to feel the warmth of another's skin. To feel the pulse of another heartbeat, to know that *she* was alive.

His hands shifted from the stick to her shoulders and he lifted her from the awkward position of leaning across the table. For a few seconds, they stood there, barely a foot apart. She watched myriad emotions play across his face, as if he were arguing with himself about whether he should kiss her. It crossed her mind to say something. It crossed her mind to run. This attraction they felt was nothing but wrong, but curiosity and need warred with common sense. This entire night had been an experiment of sorts for her. A return to life. To people. She didn't want to stop. She almost couldn't stop. She needed him to kiss her as much as she wanted it.

Slowly his head descended, as if he were giving her plenty of time to step back. She considered it, but stayed frozen, mesmerized, hoping, and in seconds his mouth met hers.

A tsunami of need flooded her, a yearning so strong she shook from it. His hands smoothed from her shoulders, down her back to her hips and nudged her closer. The longing to be held, to be loved, to be touched percolated through her. He satisfied it with another nudge that brought her fully against him. Her breasts nestled against his chest, pebbling her nipples. His mouth moved over hers simply, smoothly, and temptation turned into action as her mouth instinctively opened under his and he deepened the kiss.

Desire thundered through her. Warm, wet need. Her limbs weakened. Her breath hitched. And her brain clicked on again, like a light switch being flipped in a dark, dangerous room.

This is wrong! This is wrong! This is wrong!

The words were a litany in her brain. Not only was she not ready for anything beyond a chaste, experimental kiss, but the night before she'd sensed there was something wrong in his behavior. Something he wanted from her. Or maybe that he was trying to trick her. She shouldn't be kissing him, clouding the issues.

The sound of someone clearing her throat entered the room and Whitney jumped back like a guilty teenager.

Joni Johnson, the girl who had served

dinner, stood by the door. "I'm sorry to disturb you, Mr. Andreas, but Mrs. Tucker asked me to get you. The baby is sick."

CHAPTER FIVE

DARIUS AND WHITNEY raced behind Joni, who led them up the back steps. When they reached the nursery, Darius pushed ahead, not caring about decorum, and ran into the room.

Gino lay in the crib, crying. Darius reached down and scooped the little boy into his arms. "Hey, little guy. What's up?"

"I've already called the pediatrician," Mrs. Tucker said, wringing her hands. "He said he'd be here as soon as he can."

Gino snuggled against Darius and cried harder.

"I couldn't get him to drink his evening bottle and now he won't stop crying." Mrs. Tucker's voice was strained and anxious. "I'm not a nanny and my only child is over thirty. It's been so long since I cared for a baby that I have no idea what's wrong."

Whitney peered at Gino over Darius's shoulder. "Can I hold him?"

Darius caught her gaze and the instant he did, he regretted it. Thoughts of their kiss devoured his mind and desire arched between them. He couldn't believe he'd broken the promise he'd made to himself not to kiss her, but he had. Part of him wasn't sorry. They had chemistry that just wouldn't quit and if they were in a position to pursue it they'd probably set his bedroom on fire. He couldn't resist a taste.

But they weren't in a position to pursue it, and there would be consequences. Especially for this little boy if he didn't handle the situation correctly.

He swallowed and handed Gino to her. "Here."

After laying the baby across her arm, she studied his face, pressed her hand to his forehead, looked into his mouth. "I think he's getting a tooth."

Furious that she could be so flippant, Darius pinned her with a hard stare. "I think we should let the pediatrician decide."

"Oh, of course!" she said, handing the baby back to him. "I'm just saying that there's no reason for us to panic while we wait for the doctor to arrive."

Mrs. Tucker visibly relaxed. "I should have thought of that. But it's just been so long since I've had kids." She sank into the rocker. "If I may make a suggestion, sir, I think we should get a nanny here as soon as possible." She sighed heavily, as if having trouble getting her breathing to regulate, and Darius realized just how worried poor Mrs. Tucker had been.

But his eyes narrowed in on Whitney, the woman he shared custody with, and he suddenly wondered how she knew so much about babies. She'd said she'd been married, but she hadn't mentioned children. If she'd had them and her husband had gotten custody, there had to be a reason for that. If there was something god-awful in her past that made her husband a better candidate to have her children than she was, he wanted to know what it was.

"I'll just go back to the kitchen, then," Mrs. Tucker announced, rising from the rocker and heading for the door.

"Sure," Darius said. "We'll be fine." Plus, he wanted some time alone with Whitney. Since the day they'd met at her dad's office, he'd been so preoccupied with getting along with her that he'd let all the inconsistencies in her life slide. That ended here. That ended now.

Darius sat on the rocker. Gino snuggled

against him, sniffling, but relaxing against his sweater as if seeking comfort. His heart warmed with emotion. He was falling in love with this kid. In only two days, the little boy was getting to him.

But that was all the more reason to make sure he knew Gino's "other" guardian. His dad might have approved Whitney, but his dad hadn't planned on dying. He might have simply decided to placate Missy and agreed to appoint Whitney as shared custodian. Given that she was the daughter of his friend and the friend of Gino's mom, he might not have checked into her past the way he should have.

"So, are you going to tell me how you know so much about babies?"

She walked away from him toward the window, but didn't answer his question.

"I can have you investigated, you know. Or maybe even guess. A woman who was married but lost custody of her children to her husband probably has a skeleton in her closet."

She sucked in a breath, refusing to look at him. Darius squeezed his eyes shut. Damn it! If he hadn't needed her help so much, he would have realized something was off with her before this. He wouldn't have silenced his instincts, and he would have confronted her.

"You know what? Don't tell me. Go back to your room and pack. Because I'm going to contest that damned will. I'm getting you away from my baby."

"Don't." She turned, her eyes filled with tortured pain. He could easily guess why.

"Why not? Don't want a courtroom full of people to hear why you shouldn't be around a child? Why you don't have your own?"

She swallowed. "It's not what you think."

"You expect me to believe that?"

Whitney's limbs began to shiver, then her entire body began to shake. She had absolutely no doubt in her mind that he intended to check in to her past. When he did, he'd discover she'd had a child who had died. She'd wanted to tell him, but she'd wanted it to be on her terms, so she didn't look incompetent or grief-stricken. But it appeared *this* was the time.

She opened her mouth, debating what she would say, how she would say it, but the only thing that came out was, "I had a daughter."

Darius said nothing, only snuggled his baby brother closer as if protecting him from her, and her heart shattered. "I would never do anything to hurt Gino."

"Really?"

"My *husband* hurt my daughter." Her shaking intensified. Tears filled her eyes. "My husband *killed* my daughter."

Darius stopped rocking.

"He intended to kill himself." Her tears spilled over her lower lids, trailed down her cheeks. Memories of that day and all the days after it when she'd wondered, berated herself, lived in an ocean of guilt, filled her brain, stopped her tongue, clogged her throat with tears.

She swallowed hard. Once. Twice. Three times before she could speak.

"No one knows if he'd forgotten he had the baby in the car seat when he realized he could simply sit in the running car in the garage to eventually kill himself." Her lungs expanded to painful proportions. Sobs screamed to erupt from her chest, but she held on.

"His company had failed and though money wasn't an issue, his pride suffered." She turned, faced Darius, opened her hands in supplication. "It was his third company. He'd bragged that number three would be the charm. But it wasn't. His father was angry with him for wasting his time. His brothers were making names for themselves on Wall Street and Burn did nothing but fail." A sob escaped. "He was the family embarrassment."

Darius swallowed, visibly shaken by what she had told him. "I'm sorry."

Her sob turned to muffled weeping. "Everyone's sorry."

He rose from the rocker. "Maybe no one knows what else to say?"

She turned away as her crying took her. There was a place she went, a soft, comfortable place, where emotion took control of her body. Problems weren't solved. Trouble didn't disappear, but tension eased. Tears and sobs provided a welcome release not just for the pain, but also for her tight muscles and limbs. And she wanted to go there now. She wanted to go to her own room, sink onto the bed and let the crying soothe her.

"You weren't at fault, you know."

She spun to face him as sadness morphed into anger. "Really? I couldn't have noticed my slightly depressed husband tumbling into full-fledged mental illness? There were no signs? You're sure?"

"No, but—"

"You wouldn't accept my diagnosis of Gino. You insisted on waiting for the pediatrician. So now I'm telling you to stop diagnosing me. Back off."

The door opened and Mrs. Tucker entered with a short, gray-haired man behind her. "Dr. Sullivan," she announced as she stepped aside and let the man shuffle over to Gino.

"Hey, Gino," he crooned, taking the baby from Darius's arms. Obviously familiar with the little boy, he hugged him before he said, "I hear somebody might be getting a tooth."

He laid the little boy on the changing table and began to examine him.

Silently, Whitney slipped behind the group huddled around the baby and out the door.

Darius watched her go, cursing himself for pushing her and cursing her husband.

She'd had a daughter. A little girl. A baby who was probably the light of her life. He squeezed his eyes shut in misery. He'd brought all that back for her, made her relive the worst days of her life.

The doctor examined Gino and told Darius and Mrs. Tucker there was very little that could be done for a baby getting a tooth. He gave them some gel to numb his gums and advised them to get a teething ring.

Luckily, Gino fell asleep almost immediately after the doctor left, but Darius stayed by his crib, angry with himself for forcing

Whitney to talk, but more concerned about the baby.

Finally, around midnight, he went to bed. But what seemed like only two minutes later, Darius heard the sounds of the baby waking and he popped up in bed. Glancing at his clock, he saw it was only just after two and groaned.

Still, not wanting Mrs. Tucker to have to deal with a cranky baby alone, he jumped into jeans and a sweatshirt and raced into the nursery. As he entered through the side door, Whitney bolted into the room from the main door, wearing a fluffy pink robe over white pajamas.

Their eyes met across the nursery and everything inside him stilled. He'd forced her to relive the worst days of her life the night before, but at least with that out in the open she had to know he didn't doubt her anymore. He wouldn't be making good on his threat to contest guardianship.

Gino screamed again, reminding him that if he didn't pick him up and tend to him, he'd wake Mrs. Tucker. Beating Whitney to the crib, he lifted the little boy out and hugged him, patting his back to soothe him.

Whitney stood a few steps back. Concern brought her close enough to see what was going on, but not so close that she was actually part of it.

Things would have probably been a bit stilted and awkward between them as they worked through the aftermath of that conversation and her memories, but ultimately they would have been okay—if he hadn't also kissed her.

He couldn't believe he'd done that, but the temptation had been so strong he couldn't resist. He'd thought that one kiss might take the edge off. Instead, the taste of her stayed on his lips all night.

Turning away, she said, "I'll warm a bottle."

She took a bottle from the small refrigerator, set it in the warmer and waited, all with her back to him.

Guilt suffused him. He should have been kinder with her, gentler.

Whitney walked over with the warm bottle, motioning for Darius to sit in the rocker. "Once he drinks this, we'll put the gel on his gums again so he can fall back to sleep."

Panic rose in him. He might have fed Gino before, but he really didn't trust himself to feed the baby when his mouth was sore.

Obviously seeing his hesitancy, Whitney

said, "Arrange Gino across your lap, but lift his head a little higher than you normally do."

In three or four movements, Darius had the little boy across his lap and halfway between sitting and lying on his arm.

"Now, put the nipple to his lips and he'll do the rest. His hunger will supersede the pain in his mouth."

Darius did as instructed and Gino latched onto the nipple as if he was starving.

Whitney stepped away. "I understand how his being sick would make you nervous."

Of course she did. She'd had a daughter. He'd brought up those memories for her. In the silence of the nursery where he'd confronted her, the most natural thing to do right now would be to apologize for pushing her to tell him about her daughter.

So he did. "I'm sorry."

She ambled to the side window. Though it was the middle of the night and she probably couldn't see anything, she stared out into the darkness. "For not knowing how to care for Gino?"

"For pushing you into talking before the pediatrician got here."

Her eyes never left the window. "You had

no idea. You were worried about Gino. I accept that."

Just as he'd suspected, his mistake was something she'd probably faced before. She wouldn't hold a grudge or make something out of it he hadn't intended. Things might still be awkward for awhile, but ultimately they'd be okay.

The baby nudged the nipple out of his mouth and Darius pulled the bottle away. He sat him up a bit then waited a few seconds before he offered it again. Gino latched onto the nipple, and the room became eerily silent. This time he couldn't blame it on the repercussions of his pushing her into talking about her baby. There was a second elephant in the room and he had to get rid of it, too.

With a glance at Gino to make sure he was still suckling, he said, "I'm also sorry I kissed you. It won't happen again."

She stared out the window, saying nothing, and he wanted to groan at his stupidity. Kissing her had been a ridiculous, in-the-moment impulse that he should have thought through. Instead, he'd let his hormones rule him.

But rather than tell him to go to hell, or that he was an immature ass, she quietly said, "How do you know it won't happen again?"

He had no option but the truth. "Because it's not a good idea for either of us. We have to spend the next eighteen years dealing with each other as we raise this baby. If we started a relationship that fizzled, one of us would end up angry or hurt and that's not good for Gino."

Whitney stared outside though she didn't actually see anything. It was the second or third time he'd given Gino preference in a conversation. It had surprised her the morning before when he'd said he wanted to be a great dad. But after the way he'd behaved while waiting for the pediatrician—protective, strong—she knew he wasn't faking it, wasn't saying these things to make himself look good or get her into his corner. He intended to be a good father to his half-brother.

She peeked over at him. He wore jeans and a baggy gray sweatshirt and looked absolutely gorgeous in a casual, athletic way. His short hair wasn't exactly mussed; it simply wasn't combed as it usually was for a day of work, and wisps fell to his forehead boyishly. His typically stern face was relaxed. Neither a frown nor a smile graced his mouth.

She'd kissed that mouth.

He'd held her against him.

She'd faintly felt his heart beating beneath the fisherman's sweater.

She could have tumbled over the edge the night before, could have done something really out of character, really wrong. But fate had stopped them. He'd said he didn't want it to happen again, and she believed him. Not just because his first priority was Gino, but because of the conversation afterward. He now knew she came with baggage. She might as well have dressed in dynamite. There'd be no way a man who could have any woman he wanted would go near a woman with her kind of past.

Which was good.

Sad, because she'd finally begun to relax around someone; but good because she'd panicked the night before. She hadn't known how to stop. She'd gotten in over her head. If Joni hadn't come in, she could have messed up royally.

Her priority was to uphold Missy's wishes and to do that she had to be objective. Not get involved with her co-guardian. She also wasn't ready for a relationship. Burn had hurt her. No, Burn had cost her her ability to trust. As nice as Darius Andreas seemed to be, as good as he clearly wanted to be with Gino, an intimate relationship was a totally different thing. God only knew *if* he had the ability to have one. And God only knew *when* she'd be ready to have one.

Glancing at Gino's bottle, she saw it was empty, and walked over to the rocker. "Here," she said, easing the bottle out of Gino's mouth and Darius's hold. "You have to burp him now."

Darius sat perfectly still. Didn't let her perfume affect him. Wouldn't let himself wonder if her skin was as soft as it looked. Wouldn't let his mind wander back to the kiss the night before. He'd made a promise of sorts to her that she would be safe in his company, and he intended to keep it.

"Lift him to your shoulder the way I showed you yesterday morning."

He did as she instructed, but kept his gaze averted. They really were like gasoline and a match when they got too close, and the best way to handle it would be to keep their distance. But if he wanted her to teach him about the baby, that wasn't possible. His only alternative was simply to control himself.

"Now, pat his back."

He brought his hand to the baby's small back and lightly patted twice. Gino burped.

Whitney stepped away. "He's a good eater

and a good burper. That's usually a sign of a very healthy child. He'll probably have this tooth in before we know it."

Relief washed through him and he rose. But once he was standing, he realized had no idea what he was supposed to do.

"Does he go back to bed now?"

Whitney laughed softly. "Let's hope. Otherwise, it's going to be a long night. First let's put some of the gel on his gums."

Darius winced. "Sorry, I forgot."

"You're new and there's a lot to remember." She found the gel and gently applied some to the baby's gums. He spat and fussed, but she persevered.

As she stepped away, Darius asked, "Should I lay him in the crib?"

"Actually, the best thing to do would be for you to stay on the rocker. Position him the same way you had him while you fed him, so that he's not lying flat but is upright enough that he can breathe more easily, and just rock him until he falls asleep."

Darius sat and positioned Gino on his lap. "Hey, little guy."

As he set the rocker in motion, Whitney leaned against the crib. "Don't talk too much or he'll never go back to sleep."

"What should I do?"

"Just keep rocking him." She smiled. "You could also sing him a lullaby."

Darius winced. "Yeah. Not in this life-time."

She laughed. "Eventually, you'll sing. Everybody does."

"Not me."

"Just wait. The day will come when you're desperate and you'll sing."

Chuckling softly, Darius shook his head.

In a surprising move, Whitney pushed off the crib and stooped down in front of him. He noticed that she didn't touch either him or Gino, but she started to sing.

"Hush little baby, don't say a word, Papa's going to buy you a mocking bird…"

Her voice was soft, lyrical. Gino blinked his heavy eyelids and rolled his head to the side so he could look at her.

"And if that mocking bird don't sing, Papa's gonna buy you a diamond ring. And if that diamond ring turns brass, Papa's going to buy you a looking glass. If that looking glass gets broke, Papa's going to buy you a billy goat."

As if by magic, Gino's eyelids drooped. Whitney's voice softened even more, and she slowed the song, as if lulling him to sleep.

"If that billy goat won't pull, Papa's going to buy you a cart and bull. If that cart and bull turn over, Papa's going to buy you a dog named Rover." Her voice softened again, the words she sang slowed to a hypnotic pace. Gino's eyelids drooped until eventually they stayed shut.

Her song finished, Whitney rose. She nodded at Gino. "He's asleep."

Mesmerized by the sweet expression on her face and the casual way she'd lowered her voice and softened the song to lull Gino to sleep, Darius only stared at her. "He is?"

"He is." She headed for the door. "Good night."

"Good night."

Darius rose and put Gino in the crib. Sadness seeped into his soul. He'd bet she'd been the perfect mother.

Sunday morning, when Darius heard Gino cry, he popped up in bed again. He jumped into the same jeans and sweatshirt he'd worn the night before and raced into the nursery just as Mrs. Tucker finished changing the baby.

"He's feeling a lot better this morning." She caught Darius's gaze. "I'm sorry I didn't hear him wake up last night."

"That's okay. Whitney and I took care of him."

Before Mrs. Tucker could answer, Whitney

entered the room. Their eyes met across the nursery and all he could think of was her singing to Gino the night before. The sweet motherly affection he'd heard in her voice. The easy way she'd used the song to lull Gino to sleep. And he suddenly understood why Missy had chosen her for her baby's guardian. Whitney was born to be a mom. She really would be Gino's mom. Not a substitute, not a guardian, but a real mom.

Just as he intended to be a real dad.

He could picture them two or three or even six years from now, as the perfect parents. He could see them standing with their arms around each other's waists, waving to Gino who rode his bike along the big circular driveway in front of the house.

He shook his head to dislodge that image. It was one thing to parent a child together. But they didn't need to have their arms around each other's waists. They had to be objective. They couldn't have a relationship. He had a conglomerate to run. A life that kept him so busy he'd barely have time to squeeze this baby in. But he would. Gino would become his family. And after that there would be no time left for anyone else. Which made him the absolute worst choice of men for Whitney to get involved with. Now that he knew her past, he also knew she needed someone to love her, to understand her, and he simply had too much on his plate already. He would ignore signs that she needed to talk, or signs that she was feeling sad, or signs that she simply needed to be held. And he would hurt her.

She broke eye contact and strolled a little closer to the baby. "Good morning."

"Good morning," Mrs. Tucker chirped. "Here's the bottle," she said, offering both the baby and the bottle to Whitney.

Darius raced over, understanding now why she hesitated. Being Gino's guardian was probably a living hell for her, yet she'd accepted the job and planned to do it. "I'll take him."

Mrs. Tucker put Gino in his arms and glanced at her watch. "If you don't mind, I need to go now. Two of the maids are new and we don't really have a schedule yet." She smiled like the happy employee that she was, causing Darius to notice just how weary, how sad Whitney was in contrast. "If you need me, I can be free again after breakfast."

With the baby and the bottle in Darius's hands, Mrs. Tucker turned away and walked out of the nursery.

He sat on the rocker and gave Gino the nipple as he had the other times he had fed him. Gino latched on greedily and sucked down the milk. Whitney walked around the nursery, glancing at toys and knickknacks scattered on the shelves. She didn't say anything and, try as he might, Darius couldn't think of anything to say either.

When Gino was finished with his breakfast, Darius burped him like a pro then rose from the rocker. "So what do we do now? Put him back to bed?"

Whitney smiled slightly. "I'm guessing he just woke up before we walked in. So he should spend some time downstairs."

Panic fluttered through him. "Downstairs? With his gums just waiting to put him in severe pain again?"

"Of course. He still needs his cereal and I'm guessing he'll want to play a bit. In fact it's good to entertain him and make him happy for as long as we can."

Panic was replaced by fear. Yes, he'd rocked this kid, fed this kid, even changed a diaper—much to his horror—but he wasn't capable enough to be alone with a potentially sick baby all morning.

"Ready?"

He peeked over at Whitney. "You're coming with us?"

"Sure."

That's when he saw it. The sadness that hummed through everything she did was sometimes eclipsed by very normal behavior, but it was still there.

And everything she did for Gino undoubtedly reminded her of the baby she'd lost.

CHAPTER SIX

DARIUS WAITED UNTIL they were seated at the table in the sunroom for lunch, while Gino was napping, before he broached the subject they'd come to Montauk to discuss— how they'd share custody of Gino. The wall of windows brought in the broad expanse of the ocean, sloshing sloppily, with no rhyme or reason or organization, against the shore. The scent of warm clam chowder wafted around them comfortingly, but Darius felt more like the ocean. Disjointed. Uneven. Unable to get his bearings.

Not only did he feel uncomfortable about pushing her to tell him about her family, but he also felt awful for her loss. Technically, he and Whitney would be connected for the next eighteen or so years of their lives, maybe longer. Gino would love her as a mother, and, he hoped, love him as a father. But their lives were so different he wasn't really sure it was possible for them to find common ground.

She'd been married, been a mom and now lived in a loft in Soho and worked at a law firm. He'd spent his entire adult life running from marriage and being groomed to manage a huge conglomerate. He also had an apartment in the city, but Gino had a nursery at this estate, so Darius genuinely believed it was better for him to get rid of his apartment and live here. If Whitney really wanted to make the commitment to Gino that Darius believed she should make, then she should want to give up her loft and live here too.

The three of them living together was the only way to ensure that Gino saw both of his guardians and also lived something of a normal life. Still, he couldn't hit her with that yet—especially not after the way he'd pushed her the night before. The way he had this figured, the best thing to do would be try to get her to agree to stay another week, or maybe two weeks, and then continue to tack on a week or two at a time until she realized, as he had, that Montauk was Gino's home.

Because the following day was Monday, the end of the weekend, there was no time left for delay. He had to persuade her to stay an entire week or maybe two and he had to do it now.

He casually picked up his napkin. "I'm glad we decided to spend the weekend here, getting to know the baby."

She met his gaze, her pretty blue eyes cautious.

"It was good for him to be in a settled environment—especially since this is his home, or had been when his parents came to New York."

She didn't even hesitate. "Absolutely."

"So you wouldn't mind saying a little longer?"

"How much longer?"

With her being so agreeable, it seemed a shame to ask for a week or two, when a month would be better for Gino. "How about a month?"

"A month!"

"Or six weeks." Going with his usual tactic of surprising his opponent by asking for more rather than backpedaling, he forged on. "This is Gino's home. He needs to be somewhere he feels safe. Since he spends half his day sleeping, I also think it's important he be in his own crib. We're adults. I think we can make an adjustment or two for him."

"Okay."

She surprised him so much he forgot they were negotiating. "Okay?"

"Yes. We have to hire a nanny, and I need time to turn my spare bedroom into a nursery. So, yes. It makes sense to keep Gino here where he's happy until I can get some of that done."

Dumbstruck, he said nothing.

She ate a spoonful of soup. "Layla liked being in her own crib. Especially when she was sick."

Layla. Her casual use of the name shook him. But the very fact that she'd said it so nonchalantly told him he had to be every bit as casual. Not make a big deal out of it. Not ask questions that didn't fit into their conversation about Gino. Even though he was burning up with them.

How could a man not remember he had his child with him?

How did a woman deal with the grief, the guilt, of not noticing her husband was slipping over the edge?

Though he tried to hold them back, they tore at him until he couldn't stop himself from asking, "How did you deal with it?"

"What?"

Recrimination roared through him, telling him he shouldn't push her again, but he was unable to stop himself. "Your loss. How did you deal with such a monumental loss?"

She glanced up at him. "Therapy."

He shook his head. "Dear God. It must have been awful. I am so sorry."

She set down her spoon. "Actually, that's one of the reasons I held back from telling you. I don't want you to feel sorry for me. I want you to know. You *have* to know. You have to understand. But if I really want to get on with the rest of my life, you can't feel sorry for me. You can't treat me differently than you would have when you thought I was just a thorn-in-your-side lawyer."

He laughed. "I never thought you were a thorn in my side."

She smiled at him. "Of course you did. You probably always will. We're not going to agree on how to raise Gino. We might as well admit up front that there will be disagreements and maybe set some ground rules for how to handle them."

"I'm not sure what you mean."

"Well, for instance, there could be some deal breaker things. Like I don't think he should get a new car at sixteen."

He laughed, not just at the absurdity of talking about something that wouldn't happen for fifteen-and-a-half years, but also at the absurdity of depriving Gino of something he'd need.

"Really? No car at sixteen? In case you haven't noticed, I'm rich. I can afford to get him any kind of car he wants. And he'll want one. It's the only thing he'll talk about the entire time he's fifteen."

"Doesn't matter. Kids that age aren't good drivers. We should have as much control as possible about when and where he drives. The best way to do that is for him to have to ask permission to take a car."

He gaped at her. "I have ten cars. He could easily take one without my permission."

"Then you're going to be busy keeping track of them. Because, to me, the car is a safety issue. And a deal breaker."

He scowled, remembering his own driving at sixteen, and realized she was right. "Okay, but then one of my deal breakers is pink."

"Pink?"

"No matter that you call it rose or mauve or some other flaky name, I don't ever want him dressed in pink."

She blinked, then frowned, then burst out laughing. "That's your idea of a deal breaker?"

He turned his attention to his soup. "Give me time. I'm sure I'll think of more."

"So will I. But that's kind of the point. We should balance. You know I'm right about the car, so you didn't argue once you understood. I get it about pink." She rolled her eyes. "It's a pet peeve and I respect that. But most things won't be so black and white. We're going to have to learn to discuss issues as they come up and respect each other's viewpoints."

He put down his spoon and motioned with his hand between them. "So this kind of works?"

"The fact that we're both objective parties?"

He nodded.

She smiled. "Give us a few years. We won't be quite so objective. The first time he looks at us with real love, we'll both melt." She caught his gaze. "That'll probably happen within the next day or so, so get ready. You and I are about to become mom and dad to that little boy."

The truth of that swooped down on him, reminding him of the things he'd thought the day before. He sniffed a laugh. "I already figured that out."

"Well, good. That makes you ahead of the game."

"What about you?"

"I've been through this before. I know exactly what I'm in for in the next year and a half. I've even thought ahead to the next twenty-five years. Kindergarten, elementary school,

middle school, high school…university…
marriage."

Of course she'd thought ahead to the next
twenty-some years. She was a planner. She'd
probably thought of every special event in her
daughter's life, previewed it, then suffered
through the memories of her plans when her
daughter was gone. He'd love to ask, not because he wanted to know her dreams for her
daughter, but just because he suspected she
needed to talk about some of this. But they
weren't really friends. They were two people
bound by someone else's wishes. He didn't
feel he had the right to be so personal. Yet
he also couldn't think of a way to change the
subject or even what to change it to. Nearly
everything to do with Gino would remind her
of her baby. After that there wasn't much for
them to discuss.

They were quiet for a few seconds then
Whitney said, "This soup is wonderful."

Ah, food. She'd said she loved food. That
was as good a topic as any. "Cook worked for
my dad for the past few decades. Every time
she tried to quit he doubled her salary."

She laughed. "I can understand why."

Her laughter pleased him and reminded him
of how relaxed she'd been the night before at

dinner and while playing pool. She actually seemed happy now. Relaxed.

So once again, he talked about food. "You should see what he paid the pastry chef."

Her eyes widened. "You have a pastry chef?"

He laughed. "*My dad* had a pastry chef."

His laughter scared her. She knew he was being kind, but the sound of his laugh filled her chest with syrupy warmth. It wasn't love. But closeness. Companionship. Ease. They'd known each other a few days. Yet they were not only comfortable enough to discuss Gino and his future rationally, but she'd also told him about Burn. About Layla. Now he was laughing with her and making her laugh.

And he'd kissed her.

She shoved that to the farthest corner of her brain. He'd promised he wouldn't kiss her again, so that couldn't come into play. She had to forget all about that, the way he'd promised he would.

"If we stay here a whole month, I'll weigh two hundred pounds before I go home."

"You could stand to gain a pound or two."

His comment reminded her of the way he'd looked at her the night before when she had been practicing flirting. Yearning seized her, but so did the memory of how much trouble that longing had gotten her into.

"No woman believes she can stand to gain a pound or two." She set her napkin on the table and rose. "I need to work this afternoon."

He smiled slightly and rose politely. "Okay."

Walking back to the office, she congratulated herself. She hadn't exactly run away, but there was no point in hanging around when they had no future. She'd sealed her fate with him by explaining her past. He'd even told her he wouldn't kiss her again. Yet she still had crazy feelings around him. Which, now that she thought about it, was preposterous. They didn't even really know each other. So, whatever she felt, it was based purely on animal attraction.

On the up side, the fact that her feelings were wrong gave her a reason or a way to control them. From here on out, every time the attraction rose up in her, she'd simply remind herself she didn't know him. So anything she felt was purely physical. Something to be ignored, not pursued.

On Monday morning, they drove into the city together, leaving Gino with Mrs. Tucker. Reviewing files from his briefcase, he didn't talk. Not even to discuss the job she'd be doing for Andreas Holdings in Gino's stead. She'd been quiet at breakfast, stilted, and he'd gotten the message. She might have agreed to live in the same house, but she wanted her space. Which was fine. Probably smart. He wanted her to be happy. If being left alone made her happy, then he'd leave her alone.

Eventually, she'd come around on her own terms, soften to the baby and to him. When she did, he'd see it. And he wouldn't exactly pounce, but he would capitalize on the moment and suggest that they make their living arrangements with Gino, at his house in Montauk, permanent.

When they arrived at Andreas Holdings, he directed her to follow him to his office—formerly his dad's office. Cherrywood paneling and a wall of bookcases gave the room an old-fashioned, stuffy feel, but there was nothing he could do about that. He hadn't yet had a chance to redecorate.

He walked past the brown leather sofa and chair, directing her to follow him to his desk. Keeping with the all-business tone they'd established that morning, he handed her a stack of files. "These are contracts I'd like you to review and summarize for me."

"Okay."

He pressed the button on his phone and paged his assistant, who was at the door in seconds. "Minnie will show you to your office."

She left the room on the heels of his assistant, and Darius stared at the door that closed behind them, hoping he was doing the right thing.

He met her at the limo for the ride home and immediately retrieved files to review, so they didn't have to talk just because they were commuting together. He even let her go up to her apartment on her own to pack the things she would need for the upcoming weeks.

They talked about nannies at dinner. That morning, she had called the service she'd used when she'd hired a nanny for Layla and they had emailed résumés of potential candidates. She'd narrowed them down and had scheduled interviews with all four the next day. Because Whitney would conduct the initial interviews at the headquarters for Andreas Holdings, Darius had consented to sit in on at least five minutes of each interview and, acknowledging how busy he was, she'd accepted that. Before dessert she excused herself, saying she needed to go back to the depositions from the case she was working on with her father.

At nine when he went into the nursery to

say goodnight to Gino, Whitney was already there. He was neither surprised nor concerned when she kept the slightest bit of distance between herself and the baby. He knew why she hesitated.

Still, he and Whitney were the baby's guardians and because of work that day they hadn't spent as much time as either of them wanted to spend with the baby, so he excused Mrs. Tucker.

"We're okay here. So if you want to go to your room, that's fine."

When she was gone, Darius sat on the rocker, bottle in hand. "Hey, little guy."

From her spot beside the crib, Whitney said, "He's really getting to know who you are."

Darius couldn't help it. He smiled. "I know."

"And you're really beginning to like him."

Darius looked up at her. "You were right. It hits you like a ton of bricks."

Her blue eyes softened and became distant. "Yeah."

He hadn't meant to bring her child to her mind, but with the two of them caring for a baby, it was very hard not to. Of course, if he kept the conversation specific to Gino, maybe he could avoid that.

"Remember how we were talking about him not getting a car on his sixteenth birthday?"

"Yeah?"

"Well, that started me thinking about some weird things."

"Like what?"

"Like how am I going to tell him about our dad. Or whether or not I should even tell him about our dad."

Whitney bristled. "You can't *not* tell him about his own father."

"No, but I could be judicious. You know... tell him the good stuff and temper the bad."

She took another step closer. "That won't work if your brothers decide to tell him the truth."

"I've been thinking about that too. My dad wanted us to behave like brothers. And, as you can see, Cade and Nick more or less deserted me."

"So you're going to keep Gino away from them so they don't tell him about your dad?"

He shook his head. "No. I've actually been thinking of inviting them up to the house. Maybe once or twice a year, so they'll have a chance to get to know him. There are four of us who are brothers, not just me and Gino. They might not want any part of me.

But they're Gino's big brothers. I think they should be in his life."

She nodded. In front of the rocker now, she stooped down. "In some ways, that's going to make his life tough."

Darius frowned. "Seeing his other brothers only a few times a year?"

She caught his gaze. "No. Having three adult brothers. I know you might not get this yet, but this kid is almost forty years younger than you are. And the distance between his age and that of his other two brothers is almost as great. There are *three* of you who will expect him to meet your standards." She passed her hand lovingly over Gino's soft black hair. "Three of you who will criticize his dates, expect a say in where he goes to university." She shook her head then ran her index finger down Gino's cheek. "I'm guessing he's going to rebel."

Cautious, hardly breathing, Darius watched her. She didn't seem to realize how lovingly she was caressing the little boy. She appeared mesmerized, as if she'd waited all her life for a child and now that she was with one, she couldn't stop herself.

"In one way or another all three of us rebelled."

She looked up at him with a soft smile. "Really?"

"I attended Wharton instead of Harvard."

She gasped as if mocking him. "Wow. I'm surprised your dad survived the blow."

"Hey, to him it was a big deal. Harvard was his alma mater."

"What about the other two?"

"Nick got married at seventeen."

Her eyes widened. "Now, that's more like it!"

"And Cade refused to go to school at all. He bought a ranch with his trust fund and worked it."

"Okay. Cade wins. *That's* rebellion."

"Yeah, but when his oil interests got into trouble, he needed our dad. That still sticks in his craw."

She laughed and rose from in front of the rocker. "'Sticks in his craw?'"

"He's a Texan. It's like they have their own language down there."

With the baby asleep, Darius rose from the rocker and laid the little boy in his crib. After covering him with a green blanket, he leaned down and kissed his cheek.

From the corner of his eye, he watched Whitney lick her lips. He pulled away from the crib. "Want to kiss him goodnight?"

She pressed her lips together and shook her head slightly. "I need to get ready for bed."

He let her walk out of the nursery, but he had seen the longing in her eyes.

Could it be that he'd made a mistake in running interference for her? Could she actually need to be around Gino, not away from him? Would that help her take the next steps in her recovery?

Tuesday morning, he got to the nursery before Whitney, and when she arrived he dismissed Mrs. Tucker again.

As he fed the baby his bottle, Whitney started off standing by the crib, but ultimately gravitated to the rocker. Again, she stooped in front of it, watching Gino as he ate.

He thought about that all morning at work. He didn't know if the change was because she'd told him about her family, or if she was simply growing more accustomed to Gino, but that child drew her. And for every bit she was drawn to the baby, he felt drawn to help her adjust.

If nothing else, they shared custody of Gino. She was his partner. And he needed to help her.

When they stepped into the house that evening, Mrs. Tucker met them to take their coats. "Chinese for supper tonight," she said then walked away with their garments.

"I see your love of food precedes you. I've never had a housekeeper announce the menu at the door, unless she knew somebody was truly interested."

She laughed. "I am!"

Darius pointed up the stairs. "Baby first. Food second."

She didn't hesitate. Not only did they always put Gino first, but she was actually eager to see the little guy. She wasn't entirely sure what had happened, but with Darius in the room, it was no longer excruciating to be with the baby. There were painful minutes. She still made comparisons in her head. But Darius was like a layer of protection.

They walked upstairs together and the second they stepped into the room, Gino bounced up in the crib and held his hands out to Darius.

"Look how cute!" Darius said, laughter bubbling through his voice. "He wants me." He strode over and Gino all but leapt into his arms. The baby squealed, a sound that was half-joy and half-annoyance as if he couldn't wait the two seconds it took for Darius to snag him out of the crib.

Whitney's chest squeezed. Not with pain or

fear or even a remembrance of her own child, but with happiness. Staying at this house hadn't been her first choice for how they'd share custody, but it was now clear that being here had been the right thing for Gino.

She grabbed a tissue and gently ran it beneath Gino's runny nose. He squawked and reached for her.

Darius laughed. "Take him."

She shied away. She might have been able to touch him, to experience some of the joy a baby brings into any world it enters, but she wouldn't go overboard. She liked being able to be in the same room without being overwhelmed with memories. She had weeks here at Darius's house to get accustomed to Gino. She didn't have to push. She could take this slowly.

"That's okay. You keep him."

Gino squealed and stretched out of Darius's arms toward her.

Darius chuckled. "I'm sorry, but he wants you. He likes you."

"I know. But he likes you, too." She took a few steps back.

Gino screeched again.

"Right at this minute, I think he likes you more."

Motherly longing laced its way through

her. The pure feminine desire to lave love on a needy baby rose up in her. Especially a baby who so obviously wanted her. Her heart swelled with affection so strong it tightened her chest. She *wanted* to love Gino. She might even need to love him. There was a hole in her heart so big that some days she wondered how it managed to pump enough blood to keep her alive.

And standing in the nursery where this little boy belonged, beside the man who shared custody with her, suddenly it all seemed okay. She took Gino from Darius's arms.

Darius smiled. "Look how much he likes you."

She took a soft breath, preparing for panic, as sweet baby scents and the feeling of him snuggling into her assailed her. "I'm glad we came here, glad we decided to share these few weeks so we could all get adjusted."

He shrugged. "It works."

She nodded and turned away to rock Gino a bit as he nuzzled against her neck. The panic she expected didn't come and she realized the memories of Layla floating out of her subconscious were wispy, insubstantial. Not bold and blaring, but still there, soft and sweet. She wouldn't forget her baby as she got on with the rest of her life.

"Yes. Being together does seem to be working."

"What do you say we take the baby down to supper with us?"

She nodded.

He smiled. "Do you want to change first?"

"Yes."

"Okay. You hold him while I change and then I'll come back and take him while you change."

Whitney nodded, feeling herself able to take another careful step. Holding Gino, alone.

Darius left the room and she smiled down at the little boy. "So how was your day?"

He tilted his head as if questioning her.

She laughed. "I get it. Not much happens in the life of a six-month-old."

He screeched as if protesting that fact.

"Then again, Gino, everything that happens is sort of new to you. I mean, you can't even talk yet. Just wait till that happens." She waltzed him around the room, making him giggle. "Then there's walking. You're gonna love that."

She spun around the room again, but stopped when she saw Darius standing in the open doorway between his room and the nursery.

"That was fast."

He ambled into the room. "I'm hungry."

"Me, too."

She handed the baby to him, but couldn't help noticing his still expression. "What?"

"I think we should live together."

"We are living together."

"I mean permanently." He ran his hand along the top of Gino's head, across the shiny black hair so much like his own. "The house is huge. We both love the baby. He loves both of us. Wouldn't it be a shame to divide up our time when we could both see him every day?"

She gaped at him. "You're serious."

He smiled charmingly. "It's the right thing to do for Gino."

All the little warning bells she'd heard the Friday before when they'd arrived at the house, all the little suspicions that had nudged at her, suddenly found their meaning. He'd been leading her toward this from the beginning. Being nice, getting her to agree to one simple thing after another until they were at the point where his real goal became clear. He wanted them to live together.

Well, he could ask, but that didn't mean she had to agree.

"It doesn't work for me."

"Why not? There's plenty of space. We have

a cook. We're hiring a nanny." He pointed out the window at the serene ocean below. "You're by the sea. On a beautiful, peaceful estate. You can keep your condo if you want. Spend time in the city anytime you want. And Gino can be here, comfortable and happy with his nanny."

"You mean with *you*."

"I can't always be here either, remember? I have a job that forces me to travel. All the more reason for Gino to have a home base."

"You mean all the more reason for you to keep control. You're afraid that with your schedule, I'll have him more than you'll have him."

He shook his head and laughed lightly, as if they were having a casual conversation, not a monumental one. "That's absurd."

"Then why do you want to live here?"

"Because it makes sense."

"Not to me."

"I can't see why not. Whitney, I don't want this to come out wrong, but you need this as much as Gino does. You're still shaky around him."

Fury rose up in her. She couldn't believe he'd use her fears around Gino against her. Telling him about her baby had been the hardest thing she'd ever done, but she'd trusted him! And he was using it against her.

Mrs. Tucker stepped into the nursery. "The cook wants to know when it will be convenient to serve dinner."

Whitney headed for the door. "I'm not hungry. I'm going to work. Have Geoffrey bring Gino's swing to my office and I'll watch him while Mr. Andreas dines."

Alone.

Alone from here on out because she wasn't trusting him again!

CHAPTER SEVEN

AT EIGHT O'CLOCK THAT NIGHT, after two hours of reading depositions, with Gino splitting his time between the swing and the playpen across from her desk, Whitney asked Mrs. Tucker to bring a bottle to the nursery.

She didn't look for Darius or even let him know she was putting Gino to bed. The mood in the nursery was subdued, as if Mrs. Tucker knew Darius should have been called in at least to say goodnight. Still, good employee that she was, she didn't say anything as she fed Gino his bottle.

But Gino fussed as if he, too, knew something was off balance, and Whitney began to feel a tad guilty for being so angry. Then as she tucked the covers around Gino's neck and his soft baby blankets brought Layla to mind, she remembered that she'd trusted Darius. She'd told him the truth about the reason for her troubles with Gino and he'd used it to further his plan to keep the baby with him. Permanently.

Needing a break from thinking about all this, instead of returning to her office, she headed for the kitchen to make herself a cup of cocoa and maybe an omelet, since she hadn't eaten dinner.

It took her a minute to find the kitchen. Coming from the other side of the huge house, she got slightly disoriented. When she finally found it and pushed open the door, she stopped dead in her tracks.

The space wasn't appointed to be a regular household kitchen, but looked like the kind of kitchen found in a restaurant. Stainless-steel appliances and hanging racks of pots and pans surrounded a long stainless-steel prep table that sat across from a sixteen-burner stove. Only a few cupboards lined the back wall.

Still, big or not, the kitchen had to have cocoa and milk. She headed for the refrigerator and easily found milk. When she spotted the eggs and cheese, she smiled. An omelet was a definite possibility.

She pulled supplies out of the refrigerator and went on a quest for mugs, plates and utensils. Unfortunately, the cupboards didn't hold so much as one mug, one plate or one fork. As quickly as her mood had lifted at the sight of eggs, it plummeted. What good would it do to find the eggs and cheese, if she didn't have anything to eat them with?

Hearing the door open, she spun to face it and saw Darius enter the room. He looked cute and cuddly in a big sweatshirt and sweatpants. Then she remembered he wanted her to live here permanently and her fury returned full force.

She sucked in a breath, told herself not to let her anger rule her. It was better to find out now that he was the kind of guy who would use her confidences against her, rather than later. At least now she knew not to get too friendly with him.

But just as she was about to freeze him out of the kitchen with a cold shoulder and a frigid stare, she realized he might know where the utensils were, and if she wanted food—and she did—she needed him.

Though it galled her, she very quietly said, "Are there any mugs or plates or forks in this house?"

He took a step into the room. "Probably."

"But you don't know where they are?"

He shook his head. "Sorry."

She stifled a curse. "I just want a simple cup of cocoa." She opened and closed two more doors, working to control her temper and not start another fight. "And maybe an omelet."

"If you're hungry, we can call Cook."

"Or I could just make myself something." His spoiled, pampered, rich-guy attitude fed her bad mood. He didn't live a real life. Probably never had. He wouldn't know a genuine emotion, especially not trust, if it came up and bit his butt.

"You rich people." She shook her head. "You're so helpless."

He sauntered the rest of the way into the kitchen. "Hey, I am not helpless. My dad might have been rich, but my mother wasn't. She not only cooked, but she had a job. And she taught me to cook." He pulled a skillet from the arrangement hanging over the prep table. "What kind of omelet would you like?"

Though all that surprised her, the last thing she wanted was for him to wait on her. She wanted to maintain her independence. She didn't want to trust him. She certainly didn't want to depend on him. Hell, from here on out she wasn't even sure she wanted to be friendly with him.

"I'll make my own omelet."

"No. You smeared the good name of

Andreas with your snotty comment that I was helpless. I have honor to defend."

Right. Honor. A guy who used her trauma to try to get her to live with him was not a man of honor.

"Okay, how about this? I'll hunt for everything you need and you make your own omelet?"

Unfortunately, she was so hungry that she couldn't turn him down. "All right. Fine."

He rubbed his hands together, as if he were enjoying this. "What should I look for first?"

His enthusiasm only grated on her nerves. "I found the refrigerator so I know where to get just about everything for the omelet. But I have no clue where to find the cocoa."

"I'm on it." Turning to the right, he headed off and disappeared down a short hallway. After a few seconds, he emerged with cocoa but not the mug.

She frowned at it.

He laughed. "Don't get huffy. We eat off plates every day. Drink out of cups. They have to be around here somewhere."

While she broke eggs into a mixing bowl, ignoring him, he glanced around again. Then he disappeared down the short hall to the left.

A few seconds later he was by the prep table holding two mugs and two plates.

"Here you go."

"Two?"

"You're not going to share?"

With a sigh, she added an extra cup of milk to the pot on one of the sixteen burners, her ire simmering. If this weren't his house, she'd lambaste him for thinking he could join her when he'd betrayed her trust. But it *was* his house. And he'd helped her find the dishes. If she refused to share, she'd look petty. Childish.

"Sure. I'll share."

Apparently missing the sarcasm in her voice, he smiled, and, spotting the onion and green pepper she'd laid out beside the chopping block, he ambled over to them. While she stirred her cocoa, he cut both the onion and the pepper.

She sighed. "Stop helping me."

"I have to." Chopping the onion and pepper and not looking at her, he added, "Not only will the cocoa get cold while we wait for you to make the omelet if I don't get it started for you, but I have to make up for upsetting you when I suggested you live here permanently."

"Huh!" Damn. She'd said that out loud.

Sucking in a breath she turned on him. Since he'd started the conversation, they might as well have at it. "Do you really think you can make up for using what I told you against me? I trusted you. I told you something I don't talk about with anyone else and you used it."

"I didn't 'use' it. I simply pointed out the truth. You're having trouble and the three of us living together helps you. But there's more to me wanting Gino here than just that. Did you miss the part of the conversation where I told you Gino loves us both? He could have us both. Every day. If you'd live here."

"Did you miss the part where I have a life?"

"And you can keep it. You'd just live it from Montauk instead of the city."

"I like my home."

He stopped, caught her gaze. "Now who's being spoiled and pampered and even a little bit prissy?"

Icy pain froze her limbs. *"Prissy?"* After almost two years of caring for a baby and three years of mourning the loss of that precious child, the word *prissy* rumbled through her like thunder announcing an impending storm.

He winced. "Sorry. That was sort of over the top."

Oh, he wanted her to think he was sorry, but he wasn't. She had his number. He'd apologized only so she'd focus on what he'd called her and not on their real issue. There was no way she'd let him get away with that.

"You apologize for your words, but you skate over the actual problem." Pain rippled through her again. Not because of her anger over being called prissy when she was anything but, but because for some reason or another she believed he should know she wasn't prissy. And the only way to avoid dissecting that would be to force them back to their actual problem.

He dropped the knife and strode over to her. She snapped off the burner under the cocoa. If he wanted a fight, she was ready to give it to him.

"I know you love Gino. I see it in your eyes. You might have agreed to take custody only wanting to fulfill your friend's last wishes. But you like him now."

Once again, he was skirting the issue and she refused to let him. "Of course I do, but that doesn't change the fact that you used something I told you against me."

"I only pointed out the truth." He sighed. Stepped closer. "I thought that since you trusted me enough to tell me, that I could speak honestly about it, too."

That brought her up short and she didn't know how to answer. Had he really only been speaking honestly? Had it been so long since she'd spoken honestly about Layla and Burn that she didn't know what an honest conversation felt like anymore?

The truth of what he'd said rippled through her.

She *did* need help with Gino.

And he *was* Gino's other guardian. He had a right to be concerned.

Her skin burned with shame. Especially since she didn't want to admit any of it. He'd only been speaking the truth, but she was so out of the loop, she hadn't realized it and had accused him of using what she'd told him. And the truth was that she still did need help.

She wanted to turn away, to run, but she couldn't. Behind her was a sixteen-burner stove that ran almost the length of the room. In front of her was six feet of angry man.

"Maybe I'm just not ready to talk about it yet."

He gurgled a sound of disgust. "You won't ever be ready if you keep avoiding it in every discussion."

His angry voice echoed through the room

and she realized how upset he was. She could understand his annoyance if he were defending himself against her accusations, but he wasn't. Not really. He was talking about her. Angry about her.

"Why are *you* mad?"

He forked his fingers through his hair. "Because you're a nice woman." He snagged her gaze, his brown eyes sharp, filled with banked fury. "You're a smart woman. I know you didn't deserve what happened to you. But it did and you have to get through it to the other side. Yet you won't."

"Hey! You try losing everything! Your hopes. Your dreams. Your *baby*. Your sweet little blue-eyed baby girl who hadn't done anything to anybody." Her breath hitched. "You try losing that much, being responsible for that loss, and then putting your life back together."

"What do you think I'm doing here…with Gino…with my brothers…after my dad's death?"

She gaped at him. "You think losing your dad compares?"

"No. But when you add the fact that I lost my mom only a few months before, I think I'm in the ballpark. She was fifty-three. Smart. Funny. Everybody's best friend. My dad's biggest defender. And one day she gets to work, has a heart attack and dies." He grabbed Whitney's shoulders as if forcing her to focus in on what he was saying. "I'm alone except for that little boy upstairs and two brothers who hate me, shouldering the burden of a company that's floundering. Do you think I don't look around some days and want to pack a bag for Tahiti, buy a hut and a bottle of tequila and just say, 'screw it all'?"

"It's not the same."

"No. It's not. But just like my troubles don't give me license to stop living, neither do yours. And they sure as hell aren't going to turn into the reason you expect me always to give you your own way." His eyes sharpened. The anger in them flared.

Instead of being frightened, Whitney felt something sharp and sexual click inside her. They were both strong, passionate, vital people. Though she didn't think his trauma was worse than hers, she did believe he at least had a partial understanding of what she was going through. She was sort of sorry that she'd pushed him, but not completely. The score now felt even. Everything was out in the open.

But they were also toe to toe. Stimulated. Attracted. He'd promised he wouldn't kiss her again, but suddenly that promise seemed to belong to another universe, another time, another two people.

He held her gaze. Their physical attraction vibrated between them. Their anger withered and her breath shivered in her chest.

He was going to kiss her.

She told herself to turn and run. She knew the outcome of the last kiss. She hadn't been able to control herself. She'd wanted everything from him. Not because she loved him but because her body was desperate for release, satisfaction, closeness.

But making love with a man who was virtually a stranger wouldn't give her the satisfaction or closeness she sought. Sex would be a cold, hollow, empty substitute for affection.

She couldn't let him kiss her.

Yet she had no path of escape.

Even as she thought that, his hands slid off her shoulders. He took a step back, away from her, then turned and walked out of the kitchen.

CHAPTER EIGHT

HE'D WANTED TO KISS HER senseless.

Darius stood in front of the mirror over the double sink in the master bathroom. He'd splashed cold water on his face twice, but he couldn't get rid of the weird, compulsive instinct that he should have kissed her. Not because of their silly sexual attraction, but to shock her. To knock her out of the prison she'd built for herself and into the real world. Not for Gino, but for himself. So he could taste her, touch her.

That was wrong. Or it would be if that were his only reasoning. But it wasn't. He'd also wanted to yank her back into the real world because he liked her. And he just *knew* that beyond her fear was a wonderful, passionate woman. Someone he could really relate to. Somebody he could love.

That had scared him silly. The impulse to connect with her was so foreign, yet so strong, he knew the only way to control it had been to leave the room.

He pressed a towel to his face to dry it and headed into the bedroom. Yanking off his sweatshirt, he tried to ignore the emotions swirling through him. Wanting her for anything more than a partner to raise Gino was foolish. Dangerous. *Selfish.* He was the CEO and Chairman of the Board of a huge conglomerate full of people who depended on him. He'd barely have time to be a father for Gino. How could he expect to have time for a wife—especially a wife who would need a more sensitive husband?

He was not a sensitive man.

He would hurt her.

He had to stop wanting her.

The next morning Darius was already feeding Gino when Whitney walked into the nursery. She said, "Good morning," then stooped down in front of the rocker. "And good morning to you."

Their fight the night before had had a greater effect on her than she'd wanted it to. Not only had she come face to face with how attracted she was to Darius, but some of the things he'd said to her had rattled around in her brain.

He'd called her a nice woman.

Just the thought of it made her smile. In the past three years she'd been called cold, distant, frigid. No one had seen past her pain to the real Whitney hiding beneath the surface. And the mere knowledge that someone had actually seen the real her gave her enough strength to try to be that person again.

She sucked in a breath and caught Darius's gaze. "Let me feed him."

Darius didn't say anything, but his dark eyes asked a million questions.

"Hey, I've got to do this."

He sighed. Breaking his silence with her, he said, "Yes, you do."

"Okay. So I'm ready."

He rose from the rocker and took a few steps away so she could sit down. When she was comfortable, he handed her the baby first, then the bottle.

Fear made her hand tremble as she slid the bottle into Gino's mouth. Nearly every time she'd touched him, memories had assaulted her. And, after the memories came hours of recriminations. Guilt. Beating herself up for not seeing the obvious.

But Gino took the nipple greedily and this time she didn't see her baby's face as he suckled. She saw dark-haired, dark-eyed, very hungry Gino.

She laughed.

Darius turned away.

Her heart tumbled in her chest. Darius's silence made her feel ashamed. Selfish. He'd mentioned his mother's death the night before. He'd said he was alone. He hadn't exactly reached out to her, but had only told her because it fit into their argument. Still, this morning she knew she had to say something.

Seeing Gino was happily suckling, she drew in a quiet breath, swallowed, then said, "I'm sorry about your mother."

"It's okay."

"No. It's not." She shook her head angrily. "This is what always happens with people when I try to talk to them. Nobody's tragedy is as terrible as mine so nobody really talks with me."

He turned around again. His face scrunched in confusion. "That's ridiculous."

"No, it isn't. Look at you. You won't tell me about your mom."

He busied himself with arranging the items on the changing table.

"See!"

Still occupied with powders and lotions,

he casually said, "There's not really a lot to tell."

"But you said you were alone."

"That was a slip. A way to show you that you're not the only one who's suffered a loss." He shook his head, but didn't face her. "I shouldn't have compared my situation and yours. Our losses were totally different. Plus, I'm lucky. I might have two half-brothers who intend to ignore me, but I still have a baby brother, and if I raise him he'll be in my life for at least eighteen years. I have a family."

She glanced down at Gino. "You know, if you really wanted to have a family you should bring your brothers together. You shouldn't hang back, waiting for the right time for them to come up and meet Gino. You should take the bull by the horns and invite them now. Get them involved with him now."

He faced her.

"The longer you wait, the more distance you put between yourself and them, and between them and Gino, and the less chance they'll accept your invitation."

He crossed his arms over his chest. "And you're the expert?"

She shrugged. "Lawyers counsel people. We sometimes can't see what's in front of us in our own lives, but we have this uncanny ability to think really clearly about the lives of our clients." She glanced down at Gino, then back up at Darius and smiled slightly as she caught his gaze. "You're not really a client, but I'm sort of new to your life, so it's easier for me to see the obvious."

"And you think I should invite my brothers here?"

"Yes. I think you need a chance to bond."

He snorted out a breath. "Bond. Like a bunch of girls at cheerleading camp?" He shook his head. "That's ridiculous."

"No. Bonding is finding a common denominator. Something all three of you care about. So that you can relate to each other."

The baby spat out his bottle and Whitney burped him. But when she tried to sit him on her lap again he squirmed and squealed.

Without hesitation Darius walked over and hoisted him up, into his arms. "You look like a guy who wants to play."

Gino giggled. Darius hugged him and headed for the toy box. Whitney's chest tightened and her heart squeezed. He loved Gino so much. And his reasons for wanting Gino in his life were good. He wanted a family. This time, the guilt she felt had nothing to do with her past and everything to do with right now.

This minute. She'd mistrusted him, accused him without knowing anything about him.

Maybe the same was true of his brothers?

Maybe they didn't so much hate the eldest Andreas son as much as they simply didn't know him well enough to like him?

Darius opened the toy box and pulled out four big plastic blocks. He sat Gino on a brightly colored striped rug and lowered himself beside him.

The way Darius so easily, so naturally played with Gino tugged on her heartstrings, and once again she thought of his brothers, of how wrong it was for them to dislike their oldest brother.

"I'm not going to drop the idea that you should invite your brothers here."

Preoccupied with trying to get Gino to take a block, Darius said, "I've already told you I don't want to 'bond.'"

"So don't look at it as bonding. Look at it as getting a chance to talk about the company, about your dad, about the things you have in common."

"And you think talking will fix everything?"

"No. I don't know for sure that there's a way to fix your family. But I think it's a start.

And I think you owe it to yourself and Gino to try."

He shuffled the blocks in front of Gino, who batted at them before he picked up the yellow one and inspected it.

When he didn't answer, guilt from their argument in the kitchen rose up in her again. At a point when he would have spoken about his mom, she'd been so wrapped up in her own troubles that she hadn't reached out to him. Every day they'd been here, he'd reached out to her. She owed him.

"If you can get your brothers to come up for a weekend, I'll stay here with Gino until the Monday after that weekend."

He glanced up sharply. "Their schedules aren't going to be any easier than mine. It might take eight or ten weeks before they can come."

"I'm fine with that."

He studied her for a few seconds. Finally he said, "I guess I do have enough room here that we could easily invite my brothers for a weekend."

Darius spent the first few hours at work on the phone with his brothers. He didn't actually speak with each of them all that time. He used most of it calling various numbers he had for them before reaching secretaries who could have given him Cade and Nick's private numbers, but didn't. Each opted to have her boss return Darius's call. Luckily, and somewhat unexpectedly, both did. Immediately.

Though Nick and Cade were reluctant to accept his invitation, he reminded them of their childhoods without their father. He asked them if they really wanted the fourth brother to be raised that way—never really knowing the rest of his family. And suddenly the tones of the conversations were different. Both brothers agreed that Gino needed to know his half-brothers and both agreed to spend a weekend.

He hung up the phone satisfied, happy that his brothers would be at the house in three weeks, until he realized that not only did he have to spend three days with two brothers who hated him, but also that Whitney would be spending three days with them.

Cade the rich, rebellious cowboy and Nick the brooding Southern gentleman.

Jealousy speared him.

He actually stopped walking.

He'd never been possessive of a woman before, never been jealous. Plus, he'd already figured out he was all wrong for Whitney. He had to get over this.

Before he could take his thoughts any further, his phone rang. His first impulse was to ignore it, then he remembered Whitney would be interviewing nanny candidates that morning and he'd promised to spend five minutes with each of them to determine which of the four would get interviews at the house, with Gino.

He picked up the receiver. "Yes."

"I'm sitting here with Mary Alice Conrad," Whitney said happily. "If you have a few minutes, I'd like you to meet her."

After Darius's five minutes with Mary Alice Conrad, Whitney had a very good idea of the kind of nanny Darius envisioned for Gino. She didn't invite him in on any more of the interviews and simply chose Liz Pizzaro and Jaimie Roberts for interviews at the house.

On the drive home that evening, Whitney informed Darius that the following night they'd be conducting the home interviews with Liz and Jaimie. So, Thursday night, they set themselves up in the den. When Mrs. Tucker escorted Jaimie in, Darius sat behind the big desk in the corner. Gino chewed on a block in the playpen and Whitney stood by the double-doored entrance.

"Come in," Whitney said, shaking Jaimie's

hand as Mrs. Tucker discreetly exited and closed the door. She pointed at Darius, who rose. "This is Mr. Andreas, Gino's half-brother and other guardian." She turned and motioned to the crib. "And that's Gino."

Jaimie, a tall redhead wearing tight jeans and a red leather jacket, gasped. "Oh, he's darling!"

Darius dryly said, "We think so, too."

He walked from behind the desk over to the playpen. "Would you like to hold him?"

Jaimie turned and smiled at Darius. "Yes!"

He dircted her to take him out of the playpen and she eagerly did so. But he also watched her like a hawk. Through the one-hour question-and-answer session, Jaimie didn't miss a beat, but Darius still didn't seem to like her.

When tall, blond, gorgeous Liz Pizzaro arrived, Darius brightened.

"Come in!" he said, rising from the leather sofa where he'd been sitting to chat with Jaimie.

Whitney's chest tightened oddly. It was such a cliché for the woman of the house to be jealous of the nanny that she refused even to let her thoughts wander to the possibility.

"That's Gino," Darius said, pointing to the

baby who was now growing restless in the playpen.

Liz didn't wait for an invitation. She reached in and lifted Gino out and into her arms. "What's the matter, little guy," she crooned.

Gino screeched. But Liz only shook her head and smiled. "He's tired. Yet he's not very fussy. I'm guessing he's a really good baby."

Darius laughed. "Well, we think so, but we're prejudiced."

Liz jostled Gino and made him giggle. "Daddies are supposed to be prejudiced, aren't they?"

Darius winced. "I'm Gino's half-brother. Not really his dad."

Liz blinked innocently. "Of course, you're his dad. I can tell by how protective you are that you take the job as his guardian seriously." She smiled. "And that's what dads do."

Whitney suppressed her own smile. She didn't even have to wait for Liz to leave to know what Darius's choice would be.

"Gino just seemed more comfortable with her."

She nudged his foot with the toe of her high heel. "It didn't hurt that she called you Gino's daddy."

Darius raised his eyes until he snagged her gaze. "Is that so bad?"

Whitney's heart expanded to painful pro-portions. "No." Guilt assailed her. It suddenly seemed abundantly wrong to take Gino away from Darius, even for visits. Yet it seemed equally wrong for her to simply drop her life and move in with a man she barely knew.

There didn't seem to be a middle of the road to this problem unless Darius could mend the rift with his brothers and get close enough to them to ensure that Gino wasn't his only family.

CHAPTER NINE

SUNDAY NIGHT, when dinner was over, Whitney rose from her seat and motioned for Darius to follow her.

"I took the liberty of having my secretary gather some information about your bothers, just to get some background details."

Darius also rose from the table. "You investigated my brothers?"

"No. I just had my secretary run a quick search. I told her to get only background information. Nothing serious. Just enough that we would know some basic things."

His eyes narrowed. "I have no desire to poke into my brothers' lives."

"We're not poking. We're just looking. Lawyers never go into a courtroom or a meeting unprepared."

"CEOs don't go into meetings unprepared either."

She turned and smiled. "Exactly. So my

secretary got enough background information that we won't feel at a disadvantage when they're here."

They stepped into the office. She directed him to sit on the sofa in front of a low coffee table. Carrying the thin file she retrieved from the desk, she followed him and sat beside him.

The second she sank into the smooth leather, his nearness overwhelmed her. He'd taken a walk outside after spending time with Gino when they got home from work and he smelled like fresh air and baby powder. A week ago that would have sent her into a tailspin of despair. Today, it only reminded her that she was attracted to this man. It didn't scare her. It didn't make her crazy. It was simply a fact.

She licked her suddenly dry lips and forced her mind back on the info her secretary had found.

"Okay. We'll do Cade first." She glanced down and read aloud, "Cade Andreas, age thirty-one, net worth—" She paused, forcibly told herself not to gape, and read the number on the page.

Darius snorted. "I see that little oil thing worked out for him."

She cleared her throat. "Yes. I guess it did." She returned to her reading. "He's a loner who doesn't really socialize too much, except with the employees of his ranch."

"All of which I already knew."

"Okay." She rifled through the sheets until she came to the first page for the information on Nick. "How about this? I'll read Nick's sheet. You read Cade's. If either of us finds anything noteworthy we'll tell the other."

Darius leaned back, got comfortable and began reading.

Whitney almost mimicked him, until she realized that leaning back into the soft sofa they'd be side by side, almost touching. Sort of close and cuddly.

Arousal sparked, sharp and sweet, at just the thought. It leaped through her, awakening the more dangerous longings. To be held. To be loved. But, luckily, her common sense rose up. It might not frighten her anymore to be attracted to Darius, but a relationship between them wasn't practical. No matter how much they now understood each other, they still had a baby to raise together. If they tried a relationship and it didn't work, Gino would suffer.

So she leaned forward, away from him.

"Here's something interesting. Cade is married."

That perked up her senses. "Really?"

"Yes." He glanced up at her, obviously confused. "But he didn't bring a wife to the funeral."

"Do you think he's the type to leave his wife at home?"

Darius shrugged. "Who knows? A man who says 'sticks in my craw' could do just about anything."

"Should we plan for a wife?"

"Nope, if he didn't mention bringing a guest, I'm not planning for her."

"Okay." She went back to her reading, then had a change of heart. "Maybe we should plan for a guest."

"We have plenty of extras. If we need something Mrs. Tucker will find it."

"You're sure?"

He pierced her with a look. "Positive."

"Maybe we should check?"

"No. He should have told us he'd be bringing a guest. Since he didn't, I'm not going out of my way. If he wants to be inconsiderate that's his choice."

At his snippy tone, Whitney laughed. "I see that hits a nerve."

He set the paper down again. "It doesn't hit a nerve. I think he has the right to behave however he wants to behave, but if the tables were turned I'd be more considerate. That's why

I don't expect a lot out of him. Frankly, I'm surprised he's interested in Gino. He's busy with his oil company. He's got a ranch so big I'm not sure even he knows how many acres he has. And he doesn't really like people."

"He's going to be our tough nut to crack then."

Darius merely snorted a "Humph."

"Says here in Nick's report that he owns a factory." She shuffled through the papers. "His net worth is about one quarter of Cade's."

"Yeah, considering Cade's net worth, that brings Nick in at around half a billion dollars." Darius caught her gaze. "Don't ever underestimate Nick. He'll come here all Southern-gentleman charm and manners and he'll leave with the silver."

Her eyes widened. "He's a thief?"

"No, he's a sweet-talker."

Whitney couldn't help it; she laughed. "So you have a sweet-talker and a grouch for half-brothers?"

"Yeah, great, isn't it? I've got a grouch, a sweet-talker and a baby." He snorted in derision. "Which makes me crazy to think I can unite them."

"Or a tower of strength."

"Right."

"Oh, come on. You know you're strong."

He gave her a confused look, then a grin bloomed on his face and he nudged her playfully. "You think I'm strong."

She sucked in a breath. Even casual contact with him sent her senses reeling. But she understood why. Not only was she needy, but he was awfully good-looking. Now that they were getting to know each other, it was sometimes difficult not to simply fall into what seemed to be happening between them.

But, remembering Gino, remembering how difficult it was just to be able to hold him without thinking of Layla, she knew getting involved in a sexual relationship would be every bit as traumatic. She couldn't risk this newfound peace between her and Darius.

She got up from the sofa and walked to the fireplace. "Don't get too excited. I'm just saying that anybody who runs a company as big as yours has to have his attributes."

"Like what?"

"Like you're vain and arrogant." She smirked at him. "Do you really want the list to go on?"

He rose from the sofa and ambled over. "I like the other list better. The one where you talk about the good things." He paused and studied her eyes as if he'd been thinking the same thing she had been while sitting beside him on the sofa—how easy it would be to fall into whatever was happening between them.

Trying to get them back on point, she said, "Okay, you're strong. You're a good leader. And when push comes to shove, you always try to do the right thing."

He grinned. "See. I knew you could come up with a better list."

"You're making me want to go back to the one that starts with vain and arrogant."

His features shifted, his expression became serious again. "Don't."

Awareness bubbled through her. She wanted to believe it was only their sexual attraction, something she could deal with by always staying a few feet away. But gazing into his eyes, that excuse didn't work. In a few short weeks, she'd come to see what a good man Darius Andreas was. Were she not wounded, were she not afraid, she would be falling head over heels in love with him because he was the kind of man a woman couldn't help loving.

She sighed playfully as if put upon. "All right. I'll stick with the list that reminds me that you always try to do the right thing."

"I'd appreciate that."

His expression was so intense she suddenly wondered if he wasn't telling her something more. That he seriously wanted her to see his good points because he wanted her to like him.

Her heart leapt with hope. But she squelched it. No matter how good he was, she was weak. She was broken. He deserved better.

She swallowed. Scrambling to get them out of their personal conversation, she pulled away. "I'll bet it seems odd for you to have brothers who are so different."

Watching her walk back to the sofa, apparently accepting her return to their original topic, he said, "Yes and no. We never met until we were adults, so I spent most of my life growing up as an only child. When we did meet, we didn't like each other. I was the product of a marriage. They resented me because our father didn't marry either of their moms. And Nick's mom had a long-term relationship with our dad. It was a surprise when he walked away rather than marry her."

"That is kind of awful."

He took the poker from beside the fireplace and stirred the logs, creating a shower of sparks.

"If you dislike that story, you'll really hate Cade's. His mom was a one-night stand. Stephone simply refused to return her calls until she got a court order for a DNA test after Cade was born." He shook his head. "He didn't think enough of Cade's mom to call her back. I don't know Cade, but if someone treated my mother that badly, I'd hate him, too."

"No wonder they're bitter."

"And don't forget, our different mothers taught us different things. Mine always loved our dad. She taught me to respect him." He shook his head. "I wanted to hate him." He caught her gaze. "Not for me, but for her. He loved her, yet he couldn't stop cheating."

She understood Darius's anger, but she'd handled enough divorces to be a realist. "For some men, fidelity is impossible."

He looked at the ceiling. "Do you really believe that?"

"Yes." She answered unequivocally, knowing that would bring some sort of meaning to his childhood suffering. It didn't exactly smooth it over, but it did somewhat explain it and take the burden off the women who bore the Andreas brothers and put it where it belonged. On Stephone.

"With some men an affair is the best a woman will get. Lots of women go into them with their eyes open." She shrugged. "I know Missy did. She hadn't expected anything from your dad but what they had in the moment.

I'll bet she never spent a sorry day because her expectations were real, honest."

Darius turned to face her and his gaze slid over to hers. His dark eyes held hers, as if there was something else he wanted to say, but instead he turned away and headed for the bar.

"So we get beer and steak," she said, snatching the opportunity to return them to their intended subject because the silence in the room was strained. Awkward. And she wasn't sure why. Especially since they had been getting along, relating normally, for several days.

She couldn't risk losing that. "Since Nick is from the South, I'd say some Tennessee whiskey would probably also be in order."

"Some shrimp."

"And crab legs."

Darius laughed. "Are you still trying to please Cade's potential mystery wife or yourself?"

"Hey, if I have to be here, I'm making the most of your money and connections to get some really good fresh fish."

Chuckling, he pulled a bottle from beneath the bar. "How about a glass of wine?"

"Actually, if our work here is done, I want to go talk with Cook and then call my dad."

"Why?"

"I have a fabulous recipe for jambalaya and my father has the name of a whiskey I think both your brothers will like."

"You don't have to do that."

She smiled. "I want to."

The funny part of it was she did. She liked taking charge. She liked the spike of adrenaline that formed when she had a plan to work and was working a plan. She'd been hiding in the background for so long she'd almost forgotten what a formidable force she could be. After a brief smile, she left the room.

Darius watched her leave, not missing one sway of her soft hips, one step of her long, curved legs. He leaned on the bar and rubbed his hand across his mouth. He wasn't sure if it was wishful thinking on his part, but could she have just told him that she wouldn't mind an affair?

Could it be that in the same way she'd gotten comfortable with her role in his house, she was also getting comfortable with their attraction?

He replaced the wine on the rack and poured himself two fingers of whiskey.

There was only one way to find out.

Saturday afternoon, after the baby had awakened from his nap, Darius and Whitney set him on the nursery floor. Strong, happy Gino crawled to a stray block that had missed being put into the toy box.

"Did you see that? He crawled!"

Whitney laughed. "You need a video camera."

Darius pulled his cell phone out of his jeans pocket. "Until I get one, this will do."

He aimed the camera at the little boy who slapped the block on the floor by the toy box. Whitney slipped behind him, lifted the toy-box lid and began tossing other soft plastic toys to Gino, who giggled with delight. Darius moved his cell phone to her.

She held up her hand. "Don't!"

"Why not? You look great."

"Yeah, but I don't want to be in your pictures."

"Why not?"

"Because we're...we're..." She wanted to say they were only co-guardians. She wasn't family and didn't really have to be a part of his life. But that was wrong. They were working together for Gino. Both were committed to raising him right and well. Like it or not, they were connected. Maybe for the rest of their lives.

She threw her hands up in defeat. "Whatever. Get me in the video if you want."

He laughed. "Such enthusiasm, right, Gino?" He said, catching the baby's attention. Gino patted his thighs and spouted a bit of gibberish.

"Wish we could get him to crawl again."

Whitney stooped beside the toy box and tossed a colorful ball a few feet away from the baby. "Hey, Gino. See the ball?"

He slapped his chubby hands on his thighs.

Whitney tossed another toy over by the ball.

Gino screeched.

This time she tossed a little stuffed frog she knew was one of Gino's favorites. Finally, he rolled to his knees and crawled after it.

Darius's face blossomed into a broad smile. "Got it."

She lifted herself from the floor. "You need a real video camera. Come on. We'll take Gino to your office, get on the Internet and have one delivered."

Darius scooped Gino from the floor. "Sounds good to me."

They trooped to the second-floor office Darius used. Whitney was not surprised to see he had a second swing set up beside his office chair. When Gino wasn't napping, Darius usually kept his baby brother with him.

He slid the baby into the swing and turned the knob at the top that not only set the swing in motion but also activated the music box. Then he dropped to the chair behind the desk, hit a few buttons on his keyboard and brought his monitor to life.

At first they went on a generic search that led them to the websites of a few well-known brand names of cameras.

When bending down to view the screen became awkward, Whitney leaned her hip on the arm of Darius's chair, half sitting so she could see better. After reviewing the websites for the brands with five-star recommendations, Darius ordered the camera he wanted and clicked off the website.

"We should have it tomorrow."

He looked up at her and she suddenly realized how close they were. At first she was surprised their attraction hadn't sprung up. Then she realized something amazing. She was sitting so close their arms had brushed yet she hadn't panicked. Hadn't noticed, really. She was blessedly comfortable with him. Relaxed. Content. Almost…happy.

No. She *was* happy. She *liked* him. And not just as a friend or co-guardian. She *liked* him.

She bounced from the arm of his chair.

"Okay. Now that that's settled," she said, trying not to sound confused or angry or even weepy and scared. Liking him, seriously liking him, meant taking steps, doing things.

Kissing for real.

Getting to know each other.

Making love.

The thought caused her heart to stop. She could see them making love. And why not? They were attracted and they were already getting to know each other. They'd flirted. They worked together. Hell, they'd already kissed.

How had they gotten beyond her barriers?

It didn't matter. She wouldn't couldn't get involved with another man again, especially not someone to whom she was committed because of a baby.

CHAPTER TEN

FOR THE FIRST TIME since getting Gino, Darius felt his world righting. He had grown more than comfortable with his role as Gino's father. Plus his feelings for Whitney had taken a sudden, unexpected turn. Now that he realized she might be agreeable to an affair, their attraction no longer seemed wrong. It was just part of the picture. Part of who they were. And if they continued to grow in friendship as they had been, pretty soon he was going to act on it.

As they drove home from the city the following Tuesday evening, he realized "pretty soon" might come sooner rather than later. There she sat, long lean legs crossed, her soft yellow hair tumbling over her shoulders as she worked, tempting him. Over the past few weeks, she'd slowly changed the way she dressed from oversize suits to simple sweaters and skirts. She'd also relaxed her hairstyle, as if she was returning to her normal self. And she was captivating. Gorgeous. If he didn't stop staring at her, he'd be in sad shape by the time they reached the estate. So he did the only thing he could to get his mind on something else. He started talking.

"Nick's flight has been moved up. He'll be at the house on Friday afternoon of the weekend he and Cade are staying, instead of Friday evening."

Whitney looked up. Her pretty Persian-cat eyes warmed with humor. "So are we going home early to meet him, or are you risking the silver?"

"I told you. I'm not worried about the silver, but I'm not so sure I want to leave him alone with Liz."

She burst out laughing. "Oh, come on."

"No, you come on. He's a womanizer."

Her head tilted. "Really?"

He scuffed the toe of his shoe in the limo carpeting. He'd just called his brother a womanizer as if it was a bad thing when *he* intended to try to get Whitney into bed.

"He's got thirteen years on her."

She nudged his shoulder. "Stop acting like an old man."

He glanced up, caught her gaze. "I *am* an old man."

"At thirty-eight?"

The question came out on an airy giggle and everything inside of Darius thundered to life. He hadn't flirted with anyone in weeks. Maybe months. But there was something about flirting with Whitney that was more fun than normal. Maybe because only a few weeks ago this kind of conversation would have been foreign to her. And he'd helped her get to this place.

Surely that meant he could be allowed to enjoy it?

"Maybe I'm not so old as I am experienced."

She snorted and glanced down at her papers again. "I'll bet you are."

He knocked the toe of her high heel with the toe of his oxford. "Wanna find out?"

She looked up, her eyes filled with fear. But in a blink the fear was gone, replaced by curiosity.

Oh, yeah. She wanted to find out.

The mild tingle of arousal in his gut suddenly became a raging river. He could have ravaged her right there in the limo.

And not been sorry.

That shocked him. He really wouldn't have been sorry. In his mind's eye he saw nothing but pleasure with her. No sadness or fear for her. No guilt or recrimination for himself.

This really was going to happen.

Finally, she said, "Don't flatter yourself," and returned her attention to her paperwork, but he knew she was lying. She wanted him as much as he wanted her.

It was a milestone for her. One he wouldn't take lightly. He would make sure the moment was right when he seduced her. But he would seduce her. Not just for his own pleasure but for hers, and to bring her wholly back to the woman she was supposed to be. He couldn't bring back her child. Couldn't change her memories. But he'd been helping her take steps to recovery all along. He could help her take the next one.

After dinner, he would lure her into the den and they'd have 'the' conversation. He wouldn't risk any misunderstanding. They both had to be clear about this or it wouldn't work.

Because they were now getting down on the floor with Gino, Whitney changed into jeans before she went to the nursery to play for the hour before dinner. After they ate, Darius rose from the table and immediately walked to her chair, which he pulled out for her. "Can you spare a few minutes to talk with me in the den?"

"Sure."

He led her back down the hall. Once in the den, he pointed to the sofa as he headed for the bar. "Wine?"

Because she still had two hours of reading to do, she shook her head. "No. Thanks."

"I was kind of counting on you having a glass of wine before our talk."

"Really?" She laughed. "You want me tipsy?"

"Yes. No." He winced, then pulled out a bottle of wine and popped the cork. "I want you relaxed."

She laughed again. "I thought we were past being nervous around each other."

"Not quite. There's one more thing we haven't discussed. Something we need to discuss and then we'll have everything out in the open between us."

"I'm ready."

He sucked in a breath. "Okay, Whitney, I don't have to tell you that we're attracted to each other."

That was the last thing she'd expected him to say. Rather than sit on the couch as he'd indicated, she took a step back toward the door. "And?"

"And I know I told you that I wouldn't kiss you again, but I've changed my mind. I now think we should do something about this thing between us."

Looking at his full lips, the gleam in his dark eyes, she felt a longing that she hadn't felt in years. Oh, she was tempted, but she'd already worked all this out in her head and decided it was trouble. She laughed nervously and, as casually as possible, took another two steps back. "I'm not ready for a committed relationship."

Unfortunately, he came out from behind the bar and easily caught up with her. He stepped close, toyed with a strand of her hair. "Who says that's what I want?"

Her breath froze in her lungs. Temptation rose up like the morning sun, bright and full of promise. But they weren't the only two people in this equation.

"Have you forgotten, we're parents...raising a child together for the next eighteen years?"

"We're also mature adults who understand ourselves. You were hurt, nearly destroyed by a man you trusted. I had a father who couldn't remain faithful if he tried. I saw how he hurt my mom. I won't hurt a woman that way."

"And you think having affairs doesn't leave women hurt?"

"Not if you go into the relationship knowing the score. You said yourself Missy was fine with what she had with my dad."

"I know but—" Though that was true, she hadn't meant it in the context he'd taken it. "That's different."

"How?" He snagged her gaze, his eyes bright and serious. "Why? Neither one of us wants a marriage. Why are we any different than my father and your friend?"

"It's just that you seem so sure." She frowned. "Weirdly sure." As if an affair, not a relationship was the obvious choice, undoubtedly because she was the kind of woman no man would ever want to settle down with. Burn might have wanted her, but now she was damaged goods.

She tried to step away, but Darius caught her hands. "Look, I'm the son of a man who couldn't be faithful. I'm pretty sure I inherited those genes. But even if I hadn't, I've had enough experience to know that being wealthy changes everything. I'm tied to my job. I'm tied to this life. I don't have time for a marriage. If you married me, I'd only hurt you more. But there's more to it than that."

Seeing the expression of sincerity on his

face, she reeled back her own insecurities. "Like what?"

"My dad blamed sudden riches ten years into his marriage to my mom for making him unfaithful. So he gave me and each of my brothers five million dollars when we turned eighteen, so we'd have a chance to see what it was like to have money. His theory was that when the right woman came along, we'd have all our playboy-bachelor days out of the way, and we could settle down the way he couldn't."

"But it didn't work?"

"No." He snorted a laugh. "Actually, it made things worse. I didn't get my playboy-bachelor days out of the way because I didn't want to run around. I didn't want to gamble. Or skip school or do any of the things kids that age usually want to do. I went to class, worked hard and fell in love with a girl who was one of my study partners. She was from an average family and we were in Wharton, so I knew she was only eking by. It wasn't long before I realized living with me would make her life easier, so we moved in together and pretty soon I was paying her tuition."

"This ends badly, doesn't it?"

He blew his breath out on a sigh. "About a year later, I rushed home early one day to surprise her and I found her with another man. She claimed she'd loved me at first but her feelings had died." He shook his head. "She quite honestly told me she hadn't left me because she needed the tuition."

She could picture idealistic, smitten Darius being so coldly dumped and her heart ached for him. "Maybe she was a little too honest. Cold-hearted even?"

He laughed. "You really haven't been around the block a lot, have you? Lots of life is about money. Your own husband committed suicide because he didn't measure up. It's how we keep score. It's how we keep safe. It's certainly not the root of all evil, but if you've got a weakness it will bring it out in you or make it worse, the way it did with Jen."

"So you're telling me you want an affair for my sake."

"I'm telling you I want an affair because I think that's the best way for us to remain honest with each other. We've come a long way in a couple of weeks. And I believe we've come this far because at a certain point we stopped hedging the truth and looking out for our own agendas and started being honest. It's why I didn't simply seduce you. It's why we're having this discussion now. Honesty might hurt in the moment, but real honesty keeps people from going over the edge."

Surprisingly, what he said made sense. Burn had never been honest with her, and, as a result, he'd delivered the ultimate pain. Even now she didn't know the truth of what had happened with him and the baby. Why he'd killed himself. Why he'd killed their little girl.

"You need this. You need to come back to the land of the living. I can bring you back. I can help you become whole again. No strings attached. Nothing to scare you. Just a nice slow romance to remind you of what it feels like to be a woman again."

She swallowed and turned away. It was too easy to believe him when staring into his sincere eyes. "And what about Gino?"

"What about Gino?"

"You don't think he'll be hurt when our affair fizzles?"

"First, I don't think we'll fizzle. I think we'll morph."

A laugh escaped her. "Morph?"

"Right now we're hot for each other, and you think that will burn out. I think it will simply temper. We'll always want each other." He turned her around, caught her gaze. "If we play this right we could be something like friends with benefits forever."

"Don't you mean parents with benefits?"

He laughed. "Maybe."

When she didn't reply, he leaned in and nibbled her ear. "Don't you want this?"

When her entire body tensed then softened, it was useless to pretend she wasn't attracted—maybe even overly attracted—to him. "Some parts of me."

He chuckled.

"We can't hurt Gino."

"We won't hurt Gino." He pulled away, forcing her to look up at him. "And we won't hurt each other. You've been hurt. I've been hurt. And I had a dad who couldn't stick with one woman if his life depended on it. I can't see myself being faithful forever. I won't make that promise. But I can tell you I'll always be honest and I'll expect you to be honest. When the time comes to shift or morph or maybe even call it quits, you won't be surprised. Or hurt."

"You can't tell me I won't be hurt."

"You might be disappointed, but you'll never be stung or shocked or even surprised. Because you and I will be nothing but honest, up-front, fair. And because what we have feels strong."

"But not strong enough to last forever?"

"Nothing lasts forever. And not always because people can't be faithful." He caught her gaze. "You would have stayed with your husband forever, but you had no control over that. With so many things that can go wrong in a relationship, people are foolish to think they can make one last forever. You're smarter if you go in eyes open. Brain engaged."

She laughed. "Why are you making so much sense?"

He slid his arms around her waist. "I'll give you a choice of two reasons. First, I'm right. Second, you want me enough that it's easy to agree with me."

She laughed again, but this laugh was tinged with expectation, anticipation.

"Plus we're smart enough to put on the brakes when it feels like we're making a commitment we can't keep. Or when we want something that goes beyond the scope of what we know through experience is nothing but an illusion."

"Yeah." That was why she believed him. Permanency was an illusion. That's the big lesson losing Burn and Layla had taught her. "So what do we do now?"

He pulled away. "What? You think I'm going to seduce you tonight?"

Part of her almost wished he would. Soft and pliant, deadly nervous and hopelessly attracted to him, she knew she wouldn't change her mind, or freeze and run away. "Sort of get this over with?"

"So I'm a get-this-over-with?" He chuckled softly and moved away from her, walking back to the bar where he'd left his wine. "I was thinking more in terms of sweet seduction. A little time. A little flirting." He swirled his wine in the crystal glass. "A little cat-and-mouse."

She swallowed. "You'll have me a nervous wreck."

"Or I'll make you so eager maybe you'll seduce me."

She laughed. "Not likely."

"Oh, you don't know my powers of persuasion."

Friday night, Liz had just finished changing Gino into a fresh sleeper when Darius and Whitney entered the room.

"You guys are either too early or too late. I was just about to take him downstairs for cereal before I bring him back for a bottle before bed."

Whitney frowned. She knew Liz was a stickler for keeping Gino on a schedule, and she agreed. Babies were much happier when things were always done at the same time of day. But there was no reason she and Darius couldn't spend time with him tonight.

"How about if Darius and I feed him his cereal and rock him to sleep?"

Liz clutched her chest. "No! I didn't mean to sound like it was a problem for me to feed him."

Darius chuckled and took the baby from Liz's arms. "We know that. We also respect your schedule. But we know you have classes tomorrow and you probably want to study. Since we want time with Gino anyway, we're the logical choice to feed him."

Liz cast a wary eye in their direction. "You do know he's already bathed and in his pajamas."

"I've fed him before," Darius said, the voice of authority now that he had almost two weeks of caring for Gino under his belt. "We'll be fine."

Liz was still wary. "I don't want to have to bathe him again."

Whitney batted a hand. "We're fine. Honestly."

Liz grinned. "Okay! I do have some study-ing to do."

She skipped out of the nursery, eager to

get to her books and Whitney and Darius followed her out. She turned to the left. They turned to the right and took the back stairs to the kitchen.

"She's funny," Darius said, heading into the room filled with so much stainless steel and copper pots that it had something of an echo.

"I see her point," Whitney said, going to the cupboard that she knew contained the cereal. Since her night of struggle to find a plate, spoon and mug, all the things she and Darius might need for themselves or the baby had been moved to a front cupboard. She grabbed the box of cereal, a bowl and Gino's tiny spoon. "She doesn't want to have to do double duty."

"We're virtually pros at this," Darius scowled.

She laughed. "I'm a pro. You're still a beginner."

"Ha!"

"Just go. Get Gino into his high chair."

Shaking his head, Darius left the room. Whitney quickly prepared Gino's cereal and by the time she brought it to the dining room the little boy was already pounding on the tray.

"He knows what this means."

Whitney took a seat beside the high chair. "Of course he does. Sit any human being in front of the table where they've eaten their entire life and they'll want food."

Darius took the bowl and spoon from her. "Good point."

"I'll feed him."

He shook his head. "I'm doing this. Liz maligned my good name."

"Your good name is very sensitive."

He set the bowl on the tray in front of the baby. "I just like it when people trust me to know what I'm doing."

"Liz also likes being good at her job."

He frowned. "I never thought of that."

"She didn't question us because she thinks we're idiots. She just likes being the one who calls the shots with the baby—"

Gino screeched loud and long and Whitney realized they'd all but forgotten the poor kid. But when she looked down at him her mouth fell open in horror. He'd taken the bowl of cereal Darius had set on the tray, pulled it close to him, and had slathered it all over his face.

Darius gasped. "Liz is going to kill you."

"Kill me!" She grabbed a napkin. "Twenty seconds ago it was your good name being maligned." She pulled in a breath. "This isn't anything to panic about. We'll just make a new bowl of cereal, feed him and then bathe him ourselves."

Taking the bowl and spoon from the tray, she said, "Can I trust you to watch him while I'm gone?"

"Now, you're maligning my good name."

She shook her head and went to the kitchen where she prepared a second bowl of cereal. This time, she didn't give Darius a chance to intervene. She simply sat, fed the baby, and then took the bowl and spoon to the kitchen.

When she returned, Darius stood staring at the baby, who was still in the highchair.

"I'm not sure how to pick him up."

"You pick him up normally."

"I'll get cereal all over me."

"You're going to have to take one for the team."

He laughed at that, drew Gino out of the high chair and winced when the baby's cereal-covered sleeper met his sweater.

Whitney pushed on the swinging door to get out of the dining room and into the hall to the stairs and looked both ways before she turned back to Darius. "Okay. Coast is clear. All we have to do is race up the stairs and down one short hall and we'll be behind closed doors. Liz won't have to know any of this happened."

"I'm right behind you."

They made it up the stairs and into the nursery without running into Liz and were laughing hysterically when they closed the door behind them.

No longer out of his element, Darius took Gino to the changing table and stripped him out of his one-piece pajamas.

Whitney walked over and cooed at Gino who lay on the changing table playing with a rattle. "Looks like you've got your work cut out for you."

Darius stepped back. He didn't remember volunteering for this duty. Plus, he'd been the one to carry the kid upstairs. "Or you could have your work cut out for you."

She playfully punched his arm. "Hey, you said you wanted to learn everything there was to know about caring for him. Baths are part of that. You've probably never bathed him before."

"But he'll be naked."

"So?"

"So I'm not entirely comfortable with his bladder control."

Laughing merrily, Whitney lifted Gino from the changing table and headed into the nursery bathroom. Seeing how happy she was with Gino sent a surge of pride through him. He'd done that. He'd helped her through her fear and guilt and grief and now she was happy.

Cocky and proud, he followed her into the bathroom, which looked surprisingly like a normal bathroom except instead of two sinks in the vanity, there was a little tub beside the lone sink. Beside the tub was a bin filled with soaps and shampoos and washcloths.

Holding Gino with one hand, Whitney turned on the tap for the tub. As it filled with water, she removed his diaper and set him inside. Gino all but purred with joy.

"Oh, so you like the water?" Darius said, leaning against the doorjamb.

"Oh, no you don't!" Whitney said, laughing when Gino patted his hands in the water and splashed her. "We're both doing this! I need the soap, a washcloth and some shampoo."

Darius stepped inside and handed her the things.

"Thanks."

He took a step back.

"Uh-uh," she said, grabbing the bottom of his sweater with her wet hands. "It takes two hands to hold a big, energetic baby like Gino.

So I'm going to give you the choice. Either hold him in the tub or wash him."

"I think I'd be better at holding."

She motioned for him to shift to her left and he did.

"Now, slide your hands around his waist from behind."

He did. Gino squeaked and slapped the water again, this time splashing Darius. Whitney giggled.

"I think you just wanted me to get wet."

"No," Whitney said. "I just want you to share the joy."

"Right."

The bath took little more than five minutes, but before Gino was clean Darius was totally wet. Whitney, however, was suspiciously dry.

When he asked her about it, she gasped in mock outrage. "I just have an instinct about knowing when to step back."

As she bundled Gino in a terry-cloth towel that looked something like a baby blanket, Darius said, "Right."

"I'm serious. Knowing when to step back and when to move in with the washcloth is an art."

She carried wriggling Gino to the changing table in the nursery and pointed at the door to Darius's bedroom with her chin. "You can go change if you want."

"Okay."

He turned and went into his bedroom, but decided against closing the door. It might seem like dirty politics or maybe even a little bit tacky to strip off his shirt in front of her, but he hadn't forgotten their conversation about becoming more than friends. He itched for tonight to be the night, but he hadn't done nearly enough flirting yet. Every time he tried to flirt, the baby would squeak or squawk or want to be fed or just need time.

Actually, he'd seriously begun to wonder how parents ever had a second kid if the first one took up this much time.

Then Gino laughed as if Whitney had tickled him. The sound drifted to him followed by Whitney's happy laugh and something tightened in his gut. He wanted to make love to her in a way he'd never wanted to make love to another woman. Out of joy. Weird joy. A joy that sort of celebrated their lives.

He checked that thought. Not that it was all bad. He still wanted to make love to her out of joy—the joy of finally doing something about their attraction. He'd meant what he said about keeping a certain distance between them. Not just for himself, but also for her.

He would keep that commitment.

He would make love to her.

They would have a relationship.

He would never hurt her.

But he didn't want either of them to have their feelings confused. He didn't believe in permanent relationships. His dad had taught him that. It was a lesson he'd learned the hard way, by being one of the people his dad frequently ignored.

Days later, Whitney still tingled every time she thought about seeing Darius changing his shirt that night in the nursery, and that, of course, took her back to the discussion they'd had about becoming more than friends. She'd known all along he was attracted to her and she was attracted to him, but it wasn't smart for them to get involved. They had a child to raise.

But, oh, he'd made some really good points for a casual affair. And every day that he flirted with her, touched her hand or looked into her eyes, his arguments seemed even more compelling.

When they found themselves alone in her office again the following Saturday night, her senses scrambled to red alert. He'd told her he intended to seduce her and she knew he wasn't a man to make statements he didn't intend to keep. In a way, it was exciting. Like a game.

Would this be the night?

Would he sweep her off her feet and carry her to the master suite?

Or would he woo her? Seduce her with kisses until she felt dizzy?

In other ways it was terrifying. What if this was the night? Could she handle a relationship that was only about sex and friendship? She'd never had casual sex. She'd only ever made love with a steady boyfriend and a fiancé who had become her husband. She liked commitments.

So could she have a relationship that was only about today? No mention of tomorrow? Burn had promised her tomorrow then snatched it away like a lie. Did she really even believe in tomorrow anymore?

Was Darius right when he said permanency was only an illusion?

"Anyway, when my brothers get here, I think we need to make sure one of us is in the nursery at all times with them."

She set her pen down on her desk. "Refresh my memory. Are we making sure neither one of them snatches Gino, or are we protecting Liz?"

"Protecting Liz!" He sighed. "You're not paying attention."

She winced. "I was working when you came in." Lounging on the couch in his jeans and sloppy T-shirt, looking so comfortably sexy, he had to know he was a colossal distraction.

"Well, stop. My brothers will be here next weekend. We have to make sure we have a game plan."

He seemed so nervous about his brothers' visit that she rose from the chair behind the desk and headed for the conversation area to give him her full attention. She then realized she'd put herself in a terrible position. If she sat on the chair, she'd appear distant and cool. If she sat on the sofa, she might as well tell him she wanted tonight to be the night.

She decided to pace. She'd look perplexed, thoughtful. Actively involved in their discussion.

"What part of the plan do we not have? We've decided every menu and activities for every day. They're going to want to leave just to get some rest."

"I'm not talking about big things. I'm talking about little things. My mother always said you can't be too prepared."

It didn't surprise her that he'd brought up

his mother, but it did relax her. As long as they kept the conversation on concrete things, he wouldn't be thinking about sex. Or maybe she wouldn't be thinking about sex?

"It sounds like your mother was a smart woman."

He sat forward on the sofa. "Oh, she was great. Seriously."

"I'll bet she was proud of you."

"She was." He bounced off the sofa, walked over to her and turned her to face him. "And I get the distinct impression you're bringing up my mother because there's something else you don't want to discuss."

"No! I'm fine."

"Then why are you pacing?"

She shrugged. "I don't know. Bored maybe?"

"We have sort of been stuck here for the past several weeks." His solemn expression shifted into a grin. "Maybe tonight should be the night I seduce you?"

Her breath froze. Her limbs liquefied. As she looked into his sharp, dark eyes, her vocal cords went numb. She couldn't have spoken if she'd tried.

"I promised you flirting and we've been doing that every day. What we're up to is kissing." He brought her right hand to his lips, kissed it lightly, then smiled. "Soft. Just as I expected."

She swallowed as a million pinpricks of excitement raced from the back of her hand up her arm and straight to her heart.

"You're beautiful, Whitney. The day we met, your eyes intrigued me. Such a beautiful shade of blue." His soft, seductive voice trembled through her, heating her blood, fogging her brain. "But your lips are magnificent. Soft. Kissable." His head slowly descended. "I'm going to kiss you now."

She didn't even try to muster an objection. Her breaths shivered in and out of her chest. Her limbs had weakened. Her brain had shut down. No one had ever spoken to her like this. Listing her attributes. Silkily, sexily telling her he wanted her. How could she possibly argue with that? Resist that?

His lips met hers and Whitney closed her eyes. Dark, delicious sensations tumbled through her. Warmth filled her middle and coiled through her. Unlike their first kiss, this time she wasn't just kissing someone. She was kissing Darius. Someone she knew. Someone she liked. Someone who liked her.

They were really expressing emotion.

But he didn't make a move to deepen the kiss. Instead, he pulled away.

Their gazes clung. She could see the debate raging inside him by the look in his eyes, but he didn't kiss her again.

"We should do that more often."

A happy laugh wanted to escape, but nothing could get past the lump in her throat, the wonderful shivery feeling that held her captive.

His hands slid down her arms until he could catch her fingers. Gazing into her eyes, he said, "Good night." Then he dropped her hands and headed for the door.

He was gone before she found her voice enough to remind him it was only eight o'clock, too soon to go to bed. But it didn't matter. Tonight might not be the night they made love, but it was the night she began to feel again. Really, genuinely, feel. She hadn't even thought of her past. She'd made no comparisons. She had been fully in the moment with Darius.

Was she scared? Absolutely.

Especially since he could want to take the next step at any time, and that would be the real test of whether or not she was moving on.

CHAPTER ELEVEN

THEY DIDN'T GO TO WORK the Friday Darius's brothers were to arrive. Instead, Darius spent the morning in his office fielding calls for work that absolutely had to be handled, while Whitney saw to the last-minute details for the weekend.

She reveled in the job. In the week that had passed, Darius had kissed her every time he'd gotten the chance. He hadn't pushed her to make love, but she enjoyed his kisses enough that she was more than accustomed to their growing feelings for each other. They took care of Gino together and now they were entertaining his brothers together. She'd never felt more at home. She belonged here, in this house, with this man.

When the driver called to inform Darius he had Nick and was ten minutes away from the house, Whitney rose excitedly. "Everything is ready."

Darius wrapped his arms around her waist loosely. "I've decided I was making too big a deal out of this visit, worrying about nothing. My brothers aren't that complicated. Cade's a beer drinker and Nick is such a charmer that you could set raw skunk in front of him for dinner and he'd praise you for it. He'd sweet-talk his way out of having to eat it, but he'd still praise you."

With a laugh, she pushed at his shoulder and eased out of his embrace. "We'll see."

She headed for the main entryway and Darius scooted after her. "I'm serious."

"No. You have a poor opinion of your brothers. I'm hoping this weekend changes that."

The words were hardly out of her mouth before the door opened and Nick walked inside.

Darius stiffened.

Nick's eyes narrowed.

Whitney held back a sigh. She'd give anything to have a sister. Hell, she'd give anything to have a brother. She was an only child who longed for a blood relative to share life's trials and tribulations with. That's why she'd gotten so close to Missy. She wasn't going to let the Andreas brothers ruin this chance to get along.

"You know, I don't expect you to hug. But you could shake hands."

Darius stepped forward, his hand extended. Whitney's mouth fell open slightly at his immediate obedience, then she smiled. Everything she'd been telling him must have sunk in. He'd not only listened to her; he was taking her advice.

Narrow-eyed Nick took Darius's hand. "This isn't a truce."

To Whitney's surprise, Darius laughed and slapped Nick's back. "Right to the point, huh?"

"There's no other way to negotiate."

"Dad's rule number thirty-six."

"Offset by rule number seventeen. Never let the other side know what you want."

Darius laughed again. "I thought I was the only one who realized his rules contradicted each other." He pointed toward the den on the right. "How about a beer?"

Whitney gasped and caught Nick's arm, turning him toward the dining room. "Or how about lunch? Cade's not supposed to get here until six, so we waited lunch for you."

Nick faced her. His brown eyes narrowed again, only this time it wasn't in suspicion as it had been when he'd looked at Darius. His gaze drifted from her face down to her toes, as if inspecting her.

Then he smiled. "Ms. Ross, right?"

She nodded and stepped back. "Sorry, we should have made introductions."

His smile grew. "We met at your dad's office, remember? I never forget a pretty face."

Darius caught his arm and turned him toward the den again. "Wait until you meet Liz."

"Who's Liz?"

"Gino's nanny."

Nick stopped walking. "Oh?"

Whitney stared at them. First, she wanted to swat Darius for throwing Liz to the lions when he'd told Whitney his goal was to protect her from his brothers. Second, he kept yanking Nick toward a beer, when all three should be having lunch.

"Lunch, remember?" she said, all but stomping her foot to get their attention. "By then Gino should be done with his nap and Nick can meet him."

Nick faced her again then looked at Darius. "She's a lawyer, right?"

Darius said, "Unfortunately."

Nick cocked his head. "Pushy?"

"Absolutely. This weekend was her idea."

He motioned for Whitney to lead the way to the dining room.

Nick chuckled and shook his head. "Wait till Cade gets here. It's gonna be an interesting weekend."

The whole way through lunch Darius fielded questions Nick intended for Whitney. Never before in his life had he been so possessive and jealous, but he and Whitney were on the verge of sleeping together, and he had a sixth sense that his brothers were somehow going to ruin all the progress he'd made in the past week. Whitney was a sensitive, only-now-healing woman. One wrong word, one wrong action on his brothers' parts could send her scurrying back into hiding.

This close, there was no way Darius was going to let that happen.

When they went to the nursery, Liz was just finishing changing Gino after his nap. Because he felt bad for the comment he'd made about Liz when Nick first arrived, Darius dismissed her and fed the baby himself. He hadn't intended to throw her under the wheels of the bus, but he'd been jealous of the way Nick was looking at Whitney, and he'd panicked. Dismissing Liz was his way of making up for that.

After watching Liz as she exited the nursery, Nick put his attention on the baby. "He's cute."

"Very cute," Darius agreed. "Once I feed him, you can hold him."

Nick stepped back. "Great." He rubbed his hand along the back of his neck, as if debating something, then said, "You do know about Cade's wife, don't you?"

Darius rolled his eyes. "Yes, if he brings her we're prepared for the extra guest."

Nick shook his head fiercely. "No. I was asking if you knew his wife had died."

Shock took Darius. "His wife is dead?"

"She got sick a few years ago. She fought and fought, but didn't make it." He paced over to the window. "I just don't want you to stick your foot in your mouth by saying something you'll regret."

The urge to thank Nick rose in Darius, but he stifled it. First, it seemed weird to thank someone for telling him Cade's wife was dead. Second, he knew Nick. There was a reason he'd told Darius about Cade's wife, beyond sparing Darius embarrassment. His brothers were cool and calculated. If he wanted to keep the upper hand, he couldn't show weakness.

Gino finished his bottle and Darius rose

from the rocker and held out the baby to his brother. "Here."

Nick took the baby with a practiced ease that surprised Darius until he remembered Nick's mom ran a daycare. He let Nick goo and coo and talk baby talk to Gino to his heart's delight. Then at three, he had Mrs. Tucker show Nick to his room and gave him time to unpack.

The second he and Whitney were alone in the den, he caught her by the waist, hauled her against him and kissed her soundly.

"What was that for?"

"I've been wanting to do that all day."

She giggled, and intense, primal need punched at him. At first he considered it arousal, then he realized it wasn't physical as much as emotional. When she giggled she looked young, cheerful, as if he'd all but erased the horrible years she'd just gone through, and that knowledge brought a lump to his throat. She was beautiful, happy, wonderful and his for the taking. He didn't know how long they'd last, but he did know they were good for each other. He was as good for her as she was for him, and that made him proud in the weirdest male way. A way he'd never felt before. A way that sent an odd niggling of something cruising through him. Not fear. Not doubt. But *something*.

Before he could think it through, Mrs. Tucker walked into the room and Whitney jumped back, the way she always did when they got caught.

"I'm sorry to disturb you, Mr. Andreas, but you received a call from your brother, Cade, during lunch. He didn't want to ruin your meal by forcing you to come to the phone, and simply asked me to let you know he'll be arriving earlier than he'd planned."

"Okay, that's great."

Mrs. Tucker left the room and Whitney laughed. "There wasn't a lot of enthusiasm in your voice."

There wasn't. Not just because his half-brothers were a trial, but because he and Whitney were right on the edge of taking their relationship to the next level and his brothers were ruining it.

He caught her by the waist and pulled her to him again. "Gino's asleep and Nick's occupied." He kissed her neck. "What do you say we go to the master suite and relax?"

She pulled away and smiled. "Relax?"

He pulled her back. "Making love is the ultimate relaxation."

This time when he kissed her, he didn't

waste time on preliminaries. He wanted her. She wanted him. They'd already proven they were good for each other. It was time. He kissed her deeply, his tongue delving into the sweet recesses of her mouth, and she kissed him back. They were both more than ready—

Then Nick cleared his throat.

Once again, Whitney jumped away like a guilty teenager. Darius held back a curse.

"I thought you were taking a nap."

Nick laughed. "Not hardly." Having changed out of his trousers and oxford-cloth shirt, he wore jeans and a cable-knit sweater. He strolled to the pool table. Running his hand along the smooth mahogany rim, he said, "So, play much?"

Darius shrugged. "A little."

"A little," Whitney gasped. "He—"

Darius nudged her, telling her with his eyes to stop talking. "I beat Whitney. She thinks I'm a pro."

Nick smiled wolfishly. "Really? I'm not very good either."

Darius racked the balls. "Right."

Nick turned to Whitney. "Want to play?"

Whitney glanced from Darius to Nick, then back at Darius again. "I think I'll sit this one out. I have some filings to read to catch up on my work." She nodded at both men. "I'll see you at dinner."

Darius watched her go. When he faced Nick, his brother was studying him. "I'd have thought the nanny was more your type."

Darius walked over and chose a stick. "The nanny is nineteen."

"That's my point."

Rattled, Darius broke, sending the multicolored orbs in all directions. Four balls fell into pockets. "I'll take striped." He caught Nick's gaze. "And I don't chase babies."

"Just babes."

Darius set up another shot. "Something like that."

Nick leaned on his stick. "So you're staking a claim on Whitney?"

Darius took the shot. Another striped ball fell into a pocket. But he hardly noticed. Nick's question reverberated through his brain. Was that what he was doing? Staking a claim? It seemed so permanent, so settled. And he wasn't the kind to settle. He'd figured out a way to make this situation work for both him and Whitney, and he wouldn't deviate. He didn't give women false hope, or make promises he couldn't keep. That was the rule.

Yet, he didn't want his brother flirting with

her, either. Even the thought sent his blood screaming through his veins.

He caught Nick's gaze. "Let's just say that for the weekend I'm staking a claim."

If Nick surprised Darius, Cade shocked him. Instead of bounding into the house in boots and trademark Stetson, he wore a tailor-made suit, white shirt, blue tie. When it came time to change for dinner, he simply took off his jacket and tie, and rolled up the sleeves of his white shirt. He raced to pull out Whitney's chair at dinner before either Darius or Nick could get to it. And he engaged her in genuine conversation, not asking about the baby, but about her job.

Darius had never asked her about her job. Yes, he knew more about her personal life, her history, than Cade did. But Cade had asked about her present and her future. What she wanted. Darius never thought beyond the day they were living.

"So someday you're going to be a partner?" Cade's question slid into the conversation as easily as the chocolate mousse slid down Darius's throat.

"Actually, someday control of the firm will probably be mine. Not only does my father own most of the firm, but I'm the oldest of the junior partners. I'll choose who rises up, who falls."

Cade laughed. "Oh, interesting. I love a woman who's not afraid of a little power."

Whitney blushed endearingly and Darius's blood pressure rose. Having both lost spouses, Whitney and Cade had a lot more in common than he and Whitney did. If Cade kept flirting, eventually he and Whitney would talk for real and they'd realize Cade was the better choice of Andreas brother for Whitney. And Darius would—

Would what? Lose her? He'd never cared if he'd lost a woman before. Why would he care now?

She dabbed her lips with a napkin and said, "It's just past eight. If we go upstairs now, we can all say good-night to Gino."

Though Cade was closer to Whitney and beat Darius to her chair, Darius was beside her in an instant. He slid his hand to the small of her back and led the way with her to the nursery.

The next morning, breakfast was peaceful. Whitney had eaten early and was out of the dining room by the time the brothers came downstairs. She knew her presence was a distraction, causing them to avoid talking to each other. Instead, Cade and Nick had kept bringing the conversation back to her and her life.

However, she wouldn't have been able to have the kind of serious, honest discussion that Cade had initiated if Darius hadn't pushed her out of her shell over the past few weeks. Standing in the kitchen, peeking through the crack between the door and its frame, watching the brothers, her heart swelled. Darius's half-brothers were rich, powerful, overconfident men who weren't making Darius's task of bringing them together easy. Yet he wasn't backing down. He might be on the brink of losing his temper, but he held it back and held his ground, trying his best to get to know his brothers without an argument ensuing. Still, it was easy to see he was tense. Tight. She wished Nick hadn't strolled into the den the day before when Darius had kissed her and asked her to go to the master suite with him.

He'd been teasing about making love relaxing him, trying to lure her upstairs, but she knew that if they'd gone upstairs, if they'd made love, they would have talked afterward. She would have leaned her head on his shoulder and brushed her hand through the hair on his chest. With their thighs entwined and their bodies sated, they would have talked. About Gino. About his brothers. About how he felt. And she would have soothed him. Because that's what she did best. She soothed him, just as he had calmed her about Gino and brought her back to the real world so she could love again—

So she could love again.

She *could* love again.

The picture of them together, tangled in sheets in the master bed, formed in her brain again, and not an ounce of fear whispered through her. Only joy. Bubbly, happy, joy.

She swallowed. A new fear trembled through her.

She loved him.

She *loved* him.

And that wasn't their deal.

When she came down to dinner that evening, Darius stood by her chair and pulled it out, not giving either of his brothers the chance to one-up him as a gentleman. She didn't know whether to smile or cry. He liked her. He absolutely wanted to sleep with her. But love? In the scant weeks they'd spent together, she doubted it. She'd fallen hard and fast because he'd brought her back from the black pit of despair. He'd shown her tenderness, kindness.

She might soothe him, but that was hardly noteworthy. She'd given him no reason to *love* her. As far as Darius was concerned, except for their friendship, they were exactly where they'd been six weeks ago. Physically attracted.

Dinner was spent the same way it had been the night before, with her fielding questions. Somehow or another, both Andreas brothers seemed to know to stay away from the subject of her past. Which didn't surprise her. A few minutes on the Internet could net a person the basic facts of her life. And both were kind enough not to question her about her loss.

Cade's questions were conversational. He asked about her likes and dislikes. Nick was a lot more obvious, asking if she'd been to Europe, if she'd considered visiting the Orient. All but hinting that he'd take her anywhere she wanted to go if she only said the word.

So she bowed out of the pool game to take place after dinner. "Darius and I have spent so much time with you that I'm afraid Liz hasn't had ten back-to-back minutes to study." She made a move to rise and Cade immediately was at her back, pulling out her chair. "Plus, I don't really need dessert." She laughed softly.

All three men said their goodbyes, but

Darius was looking at her curiously. Halfway up the stairs, she stopped dead in her tracks. She'd casually, happily, chosen to care for Gino. Alone. And she wasn't afraid. Memories of Layla didn't hammer through her brain. The ones that did come were soft, sweet. Easy. The kinds of things she wanted to remember. There was no pain, just sadness. She'd always feel the loss. She'd always miss her baby girl. She'd always wonder what Layla's life might have been like. But blessed acceptance had finally come.

Tears filled her eyes and she swallowed hard. A new segment of her life had begun.

Thanks to Darius.

The man she now loved.

In the den, Darius wasn't happy when Cade turned the conversation to Whitney.

"So what's the deal with you and Ms. Ross?"

"We're co-guardians."

That made Nick laugh. "Don't even think about making a move. He's already staked a claim."

Cade laughed. "Really? You're dating?"

"No."

Cade walked up to Darius, close enough to

be a silent threat. "So technically you haven't really staked a claim."

Darius's blood pressure rose again. Anger thundered through his system like fighter jets. Standing in Darius's personal space as he was, Cade might as well have come right out and said he was looking for a physical fight, not just a verbal one. And, tonight, after two days of watching Cade and Nick flirt with Whitney, Darius wasn't about to back down.

"Stay away from her."

"Why?

"Because she's only now healing from a loss. She doesn't need to hear about yours and be sad again," Darius snarled.

Nick pushed between Darius and Cade. "Hey, hey, hey! That's enough. Cade, you're here to get to know Gino. Nothing else. And, Darius, get a grip. I can understand why you're sappy—"

Darius stopped his brother with a piercing stare. "Sappy?" He was blistering mad, macho, territorial, *anything* but sappy. And he couldn't believe Nick had said that. "Is that how you see me?"

Cade chuckled. "If you mean jealous and angry and an easy mark, yes." He walked over to the wall and chose a pool cue. "If Nick or I ever need leverage, we now know that all we have to do is talk to Whitney."

Realizing the truth of what Cade said, Darius got his pool cue, cursing himself for being an idiot. Cade wasn't interested in Whitney. He'd been testing to see what pushed Darius's buttons.

"Don't make so much out of what you think you've seen. Ms. Ross and I will eventually sleep together, but you know us Andreas men. Nothing's ever permanent. If one of you stole her, I'd move on. That's our dad's legacy to us."

Taking aim at a shot, Cade said, "So she's a fling?"

Darius snorted a laugh. "What else?" The words tripping off his tongue sounded like him again, reminding him that all the jealousy, the funny feelings, the weird connections he felt with Whitney hadn't been him at all. He didn't know who he'd been when he'd said and thought that crazy stuff. But this was him. It had taken a visit from his brothers to remind him that the soft, syrupy guy he was becoming not only wasn't him, but also that guy wouldn't stand a chance with his two brothers. If he wanted to get along, he couldn't be a sap. He had to be as strong as they were.

* * *

Having changed her mind about spending the evening alone after Gino was asleep, Whitney stopped outside the den door just as Cade said, "The next time just say you want Whitney to be off limits."

Darius simply said, "I thought I had."

"Snarling and getting jealous doesn't count." Nick slapped him on the back and the pool game resumed, but Whitney stayed rooted to the spot. Darius had just told his brothers he wanted her to be off limits.

Ridiculously, her heart rose. All this time she'd been worried that Darius hadn't fallen in love the way she had, but now she wasn't so sure. The events of the past few weeks rolled through her mind. Not just the kissing, the conversations. The way they'd compromised over Gino. The way they were creating a family with Gino.

Yes, they had agreed to an affair, but today she'd realized they'd grown so much closer, gone so far beyond that, that she'd fallen in love. So maybe he was feeling it, too?

He had to be. Why else would he be jealous and snarl? She stifled a giggle. She would have loved to have seen him snarl.

She turned around and went to her bedroom where she rummaged through the things she'd brought from home, looking for something cute, something sexy, something that would tell him in just one look that she was ready. Tonight they would make love.

Unfortunately, she didn't find anything. So she settled for a silky camisole and pajama bottoms.

Opening her door, she peeked into the hall, saw no one around and tiptoed to the master suite. She hadn't heard him come upstairs yet, but when he did she would be waiting for him.

An hour later, Darius headed for the master suite. Though they seemed to have come to terms about Whitney, he and his brothers were no closer to getting along than they had been the morning of his father's death. It was frustrating and irritating, and made him so angry he wanted to ask them both to leave. They weren't really trying to get along. Each appeared only to have come to Montauk to get a closer look at Gino.

He snorted a laugh. What purpose did it serve to have them here except to raise his blood pressure?

But when he opened the door and saw Whitney sitting on the corner of his bed, like a sweet present waiting to be unwrapped, everything about his brothers fell out of his head.

She was making the move. *She* was going to seduce *him*.

"Hey."

She peeked up at him and smiled shyly. "Hey."

He wanted to rip off his sweater and jump out of his jeans on the way to the bed, but he remembered her sensibilities so he simply ambled to the bed, sat beside her.

"How'd your night go?"

"Aggravating as hell. My brothers are morons."

She laughed. "I think they both have their good points."

"Oh, you would! They fawned all over you. They're making mincemeat out of me."

She laughed. "They're testing you. That's all. It's like you're playing a real-life game of king of the mountain. You might be the oldest brother, but they've lived their lives without you. They want to make sure you know you can't push them around."

He ran his hand along the back of his neck. "Right." The urge to confide in her rose up in him. He wanted to tell her everything they'd said, all the pushing they'd done, all the ways he'd had to hold his ground.

But, with his brothers in the wing on the other side of the house, the infernal need to tell her everything only served to remind him that they thought he was sappy. Weak. Vulnerable.

So if he really only wanted a fling with Whitney, he couldn't tell her everything. There were pieces of himself he'd have to keep to himself.

"They're cautious about the three of us becoming friends," he said simply, sliding his hand across her back. "But...I'd rather not talk about them."

He said this as he lowered his head and kissed her. Because he'd taken her by surprise, the kiss she returned was instinctive and sweeter than any he'd ever experienced.

He stopped. He didn't want sweet from her. Not tonight. All he'd ever wanted from Whitney was untamed passion. Something he could easily label. Compartmentalize. Forget.

Forget?

The word brought him up short. Angered him. He pulled away, rose from the bed and began to pace. Planning to forget Whitney pierced an arrow through his heart. Yet, how could he deny that was what he was doing? All short-term relationships were forgettable. That was why they were so easy. So uncomplicated.

But he knew Whitney was neither easy nor uncomplicated. Plus, Gino would keep them together for the rest of their lives. Still, they'd made their agreement to start an affair keeping those two things in mind. They'd planned for this. Carefully.

"I take it you're here because you're still good with a temporary relationship?"

"Yes and no."

He spun around. "Yes and no?"

"Yeah, I…um…"

Nerves took Whitney as reality sunk in. A man who'd changed his mind about an affair because he loved her wouldn't be pacing by the bed. He wouldn't be nearly crazy with nerves or confusion. He'd tell her he loved her, kiss her and seduce her.

Somehow she'd gotten all the signals mixed.

She combed her fingers through her hair. "You don't love me."

His face registered shock, then dismay. But he blinked both away before he sat beside her on the bed again.

"That wasn't our deal. But this isn't a cold, calculating thing for me either. Otherwise, we'd be naked and tangled in sheets right now.

I care deeply about you. I feel so many more things than I usually feel for a woman that it scares me."

Another woman might have taken his words to heart, seen them as a stepping stone to love, but she knew Darius. He made decisions quickly, easily. If there was even a chance that he loved her, he'd know it. He'd say it.

"You have feelings, but you don't love me."

He said nothing. But the fact that he wouldn't speak spoke volumes.

Confusion overrode pain, mostly because confusion could give her the strength to walk out of the room before she burst into tears.

He caught her chin and forced her to look at him. "I thought you wanted what I wanted."

"I did."

His gazed locked with hers. "But now you don't?"

"I thought we were on the same page."

Realization sparked in his dark eyes. "You thought we were falling in love."

"I *did* fall in love."

"Oh." He squeezed his eyes shut. "Whitney, I… I…"

She sucked in a shaky breath. "Don't stutter. Don't stumble. Just say it. You don't love me."

He swallowed hard.

She shook her head and sprang from the bed, racing to the door, eager to get away as tears rimmed her eyelids.

He jumped up and followed her. "This isn't about you or me. My father—"

She spun around. "Don't!" Her sharp voice stopped him. "Don't come after me and don't blame this on your family, your genes. This isn't about genes. It's about choices. Your dad might have been a runaround, but that was his choice. You said we were going to build this relationship on honesty. Then you can at least be man enough to say you don't like me enough to choose me."

"You don't understand—"

"No. *You* don't understand. If you loved me, you wouldn't be able to resist. A commitment wouldn't scare you. So, no, Darius, you do not love me."

With that she walked out of the room. Pain dulled her senses, but not her brain. She slipped into the nursery where she quietly packed Gino's duffel and diaper bags. She gathered his bottles and cereal from the kitchen. Then she woke Darius's driver and Liz. Before the sun rose, she and Liz were in the living room of her Soho loft and Gino slept soundly in his carrier.

CHAPTER TWELVE

DARIUS WOKE THE NEXT MORNING feeling like a man with a hangover. His head ached. His eyes thumped. Every muscle in his body hurt. He knew he hadn't had enough to drink to make him feel like a man who'd been run over by a train. Lack of sleep most likely had caused the aches and pains and thumping.

After his fight with Whitney, after she'd stormed out, he'd gone to the shower, hoping to give her twenty minutes or so to calm down before they talked again. He stood under the cold water for God only knew how long. But he'd had to spend a lot more time than he'd anticipated for the arousal thundering through his blood to dissipate. By the time it had and he returned to his bedroom, the house was quiet.

Relief had fluttered through him. He'd hated having hurt her, but he knew that if she'd fallen asleep that easily she'd be fine.

Of course, he'd also realized that she could be awake across the hall and he wouldn't hear her. So he'd paced, listened for sounds that she was awake, listened for any indication that she'd gone downstairs for cocoa. Hoping they could talk again. But he'd never heard a sound.

That's when he'd started dealing with memories. She'd been everywhere in his house, even his bedroom. He could picture her laughing, frightened, courageously walking over to take Gino from Liz. And every memory seared his heart, made him feel like a bastard for leading her on. But he hadn't led her on. He'd been honest. Fair. She was the one who'd broken their deal.

Now, *he* had to deal with the mess that caused. All the while she'd be two steps away, or a few rooms away. And the pain evident on her face would be his fault this time. Not a dead husband's.

He slid out of bed and into sweatpants and a T-shirt and forced himself into the nursery. Liz was nowhere around and the crib was empty. He hated the relief that flooded him at the obvious reprieve he was getting, until he saw an envelope leaning against a stuffed bear on the dresser. He walked over to it and opened it.

I've changed my mind about living at Montauk. I've taken Gino and Liz to the city. You may, of course, visit any time. Simply call before you want to see Gino. We'll see my father to get a custody agreement drawn up.
Whitney

Darius expected anger to roll through him. How dare she take the baby? Instead of anger, though, something squeezed his heart.

Before he could even think about that, the nursery door opened. Nick stepped inside and immediately walked to the crib. "Where's the baby?"

The nursery door opened again. This time Cade walked in. "Hey." He glanced at the crib. "Where's Gino?"

Darius waved the note. "Apparently Whitney took him back to the city."

Both Nick and Cade glanced over at him. Nick's eyebrows rose. Cade frowned. "What did you do?"

Darius tossed the note to the dresser. "What makes you think I did something?"

"Because that line you fed us last night about only wanting to sleep with her was pure rubbish."

Nick laughed. "Right. That was really kind of priceless."

Cade all but rolled with laughter. "I know! Any idiot could see he was smitten."

Fury at both of them rumbled through Darius like thunder before a dangerous storm.

"I was not smitten."

Nick said, "You were."

"And what makes the two of you experts? We are all three Andreas men. I know how we are."

Nick shook his head with a chuckle. "You keep telling yourself that. You keep telling yourself that you can't love her or be faithful or whatever it is you tell yourself and see how far that gets you."

Whitney awakened around ten to sunlight filtering in through the wall of windows in her condo bedroom and the sound of Gino crying. She popped up and was at the drawer-made-crib beside her bed in seconds, hoping not to disturb Liz.

"Hey little guy," she crooned, reaching for a clean diaper. "Just let me take care of this and we'll get a bottle."

Liz groggily walked into the room. "I'll get the bottle."

"I'm fine. Why don't you go back to sleep?"

Liz looked at her compassionately. "We're both exhausted. So why don't we share duties until we can both get a nap?"

Whitney smiled. Now that Darius had helped her out of her grief, it didn't seem wrong to accept another person's help. "Okay."

Liz left the room and Whitney changed Gino's diaper. Knowing Liz would need a minute to warm the bottle, she lifted Gino out of the drawer and held him. Close. Because she could. Because she was stronger now.

But memories of the days she'd spent with Gino and Darius assaulted her. She couldn't believe a man who'd so sensitively brought her back to life could believe he wasn't capable of fidelity…of love.

It made no sense, but she wasn't a dewy-eyed schoolgirl anymore. Darius had been very plain and very clear in his intentions. She was the one who'd gone too far.

And now she was paying the price. She might be stronger. She might finally have the ability to love again. But being able to love had put her in the line of fire for another kind of heartache.

Different from having lost Burn and Layla, this pain rattled through her like a restless ghost with a chain, called her a fool, reminded her that loneliness took many forms, reminded her that when Darius could have chosen her, he'd stepped away, not even wanting to try.

CHAPTER THIRTEEN

SUNDAY MORNING, after walking his brothers to the limo that would take them to the airport, Darius stepped into his huge house and closed the door. The front foyer echoed around him. Empty. Hollow.

He knew the feeling because it mimicked the one in his chest. He swore that without Gino in the nursery and Whitney working in the first-floor office, there was a hole where his heart should be.

Which was foolish. He was damned near forty. With the exception of Jen, he'd never had a relationship that had lasted over four months. He was a scoundrel. A louse. He'd hurt Whitney because he'd selfishly assumed they were on the same page romantically. True, they'd had an agreement but he should have seen the signs that she wanted something more. He should have realized she was falling in love. He knew she was delicate. He knew she deserved something more. Yet, he'd selfishly barreled on, seeking only what he wanted.

He should be shot. Not coddled. So he forced himself to work that afternoon. He took his dinner in the office because after trying to eat lunch alone, with only the ocean view for company, he felt like a man who'd been beaten with a club. He didn't want to miss Whitney, didn't deserve to miss Whitney, but he did.

Monday morning in the limo, he thought about the day he kept bumping toes with her and he laughed, then his chest seized with pain. She brought out the stupidest damned urges in him. He should be glad she was gone. Glad he'd dodged the bullet. Glad he hadn't actually slept with her and really hurt her.

Instead all he felt was lonely. Hurt. Alone.

On Thursday, after having spent the week at the office avoiding her, he realized he could get Gino for the weekend. That lifted his spirits, but the fact that he'd have to talk to Whitney to get permission lifted them more.

He told himself that was stupid as he walked down the hall to her office. It was best for the two of them to stay out of each other's way until the whole heartache thing was over with. He shouldn't want to see her. Still, he wanted Gino for the weekend and he was halfway to her office.

So he continued down the corridor, but as he stepped into her office he saw her desk was empty.

Her assistant walked up behind him. "She now works afternoons for Montgomery, Ross and Swaggart."

"The deal was—"

Maisey Lenosky, a tall brunette who'd worked for his dad for decades, looked at him over the top of her glasses. "If you're not happy, take this up with her. I'm not your go-between. But trust me, had I been in her shoes I'd have gone, too."

Fear sliced through him. "She told you?"

"She didn't have to. I could see for myself you hadn't given her any work all week. So she went back to the job that did."

Relief replaced the fear in a dizzying wave. "Oh. Okay. I'll call her."

He didn't wait for Maisey's reply, simply headed for his office. He dialed the number for Whitney's cell phone and immediately went to voice mail. So he dialed the firm and asked to be put through to her. Instead he got her assistant.

If it were anyone other than Whitney, he'd wonder about getting the run-around. But she was too serious, too honest, to dodge him. She would know he was calling to make arrangements for Gino and she'd accommodate him.

"I'd like Ms. Ross to call me back."

"May I ask what this is about?"

He wanted to say no, if only because it annoyed him to be jumping through hoops with staff, but he said, "Yes. We share custody of my half-brother. I would like to take him to my house in Montauk this weekend."

"That's great. I'll give her the message."

Ten minutes later, Whitney's assistant called back. "She says you may pick up Gino at six on Friday night and keep him until Sunday at about six."

Affront charged through him that she hadn't called him back, but he remembered that he'd hurt her and decided that this was the treatment he deserved. But on Friday night he intended to talk to her. To tell her he was sorry. Truly sorry. So that she could move on. So *they* could move on.

Friday night, Liz answered the concierge call that let him up to Whitney's apartment. He tried not to be on pins and needles about seeing Whitney again, but it was no use. He desperately wanted to ease the pain of the hurt he'd caused her.

So when he stepped into the apartment and Liz immediately handed him the diaper bag and headed for the door, he stopped dead in his tracks. "Where's Whitney?"

"Dinner with her parents. She just left." Liz smiled patiently. "And I'd like to get going so I can get a few hours to study tonight."

He took the hint and left the apartment, following Liz to his limo. But the weekend without Whitney was strained. Though Liz was bright and perky and very happy to stay and play with Gino and Darius the way Whitney had, it wasn't the same.

At night, he stared out the window at the dark ocean, brooding, angry with himself. What made him different from his father was that he didn't hurt the women he romanced. And he hadn't intended to this time, but he had, and that knowledge kicked around inside him. His chest ached. His soul mourned. He wasn't the kind of man who hurt women. Knowing that he had hurt Whitney was killing him.

Sunday night, Whitney wasn't around when he returned Liz and Gino to her apartment. He'd expected that. If he were angry with himself for how he treated Whitney, then how could he expect Whitney to be any less so?

Monday morning, he dressed carefully. Dark suit, white shirt, red tie. It was the first time in his adult life he could remember being worried about his appearance, but concern over the way that he'd hurt Whitney was eating him up. He longed to apologize, to make things right, and this morning he would so that he could get rid of this awful pain.

But when he reached Whitney's office, Maisey sat behind her desk.

"Where's Whitney?"

"She switched her schedule." Maisey sat forward, smiling at him. "In fact, even she isn't sure what days she's working mornings and what days she's working afternoons."

"She's avoiding me."

"No, actually, her father has given her lead chair in a civil suit. She's very excited."

So was he. He knew how much she loved her work. "Really! That's great."

"She's like a kid at Christmas."

That did not hit him as happily as the first comment did. She wasn't missing him. Didn't care that he was out of her life. Not that he wanted her to be suffering. So this news should have made him feel better. Instead, he felt worse. Rumpled. As if he were an old shirt she'd taken off, rolled into a ball and tossed into the laundry.

Which was foolish. He wanted her to be happy. So why did the news that she was moving on make him feel worse?

Tuesday, he didn't go to work. He took the important phone calls at home and spent most of his day reading financial reports. He didn't shave. He didn't eat. The dining room was now an unholy place of torment. There was no baby to amuse him, no conversation to offset the sound of the pounding surf.

Wednesday morning, he was again in his home office, supposedly reading, but actually alternating between staring at the fire and staring at the ocean. It took him completely by surprise when Mrs. Tucker entered the room.

"You have a phone call."

"I told you I'm not taking calls."

"It's your brother." She smiled. "The sweet-talker."

Darius sighed. "That would be Nick."

She left the room and he yanked the phone from the cradle. "What do you want?"

"Oh, touchy."

"I don't have time to horse around Nick. I have—" Actually, he had nothing. He couldn't focus. He didn't want to focus. He didn't know what he wanted.

"You miss her."

Of course he missed her. What an asinine statement. "I hurt her."

Nick had the audacity to laugh. "Oh, Darius. It sounds like she hurt you more."

"I feel bad because I know I made her feel bad."

"Really?"

"Yes."

"You don't feel bad yourself?"

"Of course I feel bad. I just told you. I hate that I hurt her."

"And that's what's making you stay home?"

"That and the fact that I don't want to shave."

Nick laughed merrily. "Darius! Have you never had your heart broken before? You sound just like me when my ex-wife Maggie left. I couldn't eat. I couldn't sleep. I stared at the damned ocean all day."

Darius said nothing.

"Is that what you're doing?"

Darius scowled.

"Darius?"

"Yes, all right!" Darius snarled. "I've been at home for two days, not shaving, not eating, staring at the ocean. Let's not make a big deal out of it."

"Why not?"

Why not? Darius was just about to slam down the phone or thunder a retort, until he realized he had no retort. He ached. He missed Whitney. Not the way he'd miss a girl-friend who couldn't make it to the house for a weekend. Not the way he missed a lover who'd brushed him off. But like…like part of his life. When she'd walked out the door, his future had changed. He hadn't realized it, but in the weeks they had lived together, he had begun to picture Whitney helping him raise Gino. He'd seen them as Gino's parents. He'd seen them together, happy, for years…without even realizing he was doing it.

He missed her, longed for her, because she was the part of himself he'd been missing. And he finally saw that maybe, just maybe, he hadn't been a philanderer because he liked women—well, that was part of it. But in real-ity, after Jen had hurt him, he hadn't wanted to go through that pain again, so he'd been biding his time, entertaining himself, until he found the right woman. Someone he could trust with his heart.

And he'd found her.

He'd found the right woman.

And he'd lost her.

"Go get her."

Nick's advice sounded so simple, so easy. But Darius knew better. Or maybe he didn't. After Jen, he'd never wanted a woman back, never tried to get one back. He had no frame of reference for what to expect. She could welcome him with open arms. She could slash him to ribbons. Worse, she simply might not want him. She'd said she loved him, but what if he'd killed that love?

Intense pain rumbled through him. Seized his lungs. Burned his soul. He'd never gone to a woman without the confidence of knowing she wanted him. He'd be laid bare. Defenseless. He wasn't sure he could do it.

"She's lead chair in a big civil suit. I can't just walk into a courthouse and pluck her out. Especially since I haven't shaved."

"How about this?" Nick said, his voice unexpectedly kind. "Shower, shave and stop at a florist. Buy an armload of roses. Then go to her apartment. Liz is there with the baby, right?"

"Yes."

"Well, Liz will let you in and Whitney's got to get there sometime."

That was true. "If I know Whitney, she won't work late. She might bring two armloads

of files home, but she'll get home on time, re-
lieve Liz, spend time with Gino, then she'll
work."

"So now you know what time to go. Don't
spend the rest of the day brooding. Think
about what you'll say, but don't over-rehearse."
Nick paused. "And call me tomorrow and let
me know how it went."

Darius blinked. Had Nick just asked him
to call him?

It had never occurred to Darius that having
his brother's support would lift his spirits or
give him a weird kind of courage, but it did.
"Okay. I will." He stumbled over the agreement, but when it came out it was surprisingly
easy. "Thanks."

Whitney took a cab from the office to her
home. She yanked out two briefcases full of
work, set them beside her on the sidewalk and
paid the driver.

When she turned, Jake, the young concierge, was lifting her briefcases. "Evening,
Ms. Ross."

"Good evening, Jake."

There was a gleam in his eye. An unholy
sparkle. The force of it hit Whitney in the
stomach and sent little pricks of misery
through her. Jake liked Liz. Liz liked Jake.

They were about the same age, both attending university. They were a good match. She should have been happy.

Instead, their attraction reminded her of how foolish she'd been.

"I'll ride with you," Jake said, when Whitney attempted to take the briefcases as they reached the elevator.

She smiled. "Of course. Thank you." She wouldn't punish Jake for being a good guy who'd found a girl he really meshed with. But she would continue to remind herself that it had been stupidity to think the likes of Darius Andreas would fall for her and commit. She'd genuinely believed he'd fallen. But he hadn't. She had to get over that.

And she would. After she wallowed in misery for a few weeks over Darius. But that was good. It would teach her not to be so naive again.

When she opened her apartment door, the scent of clam chowder greeted her. Her mouth watered. By the time she turned around to thank Jake, he was gone. Her two briefcases sat in the open doorway, but he was nowhere in sight.

She grabbed the briefcases and pulled them into the condo, toward the table where she would work. "Liz?"

No answer. She walked to the kitchen area and snapped off the burner beneath the bubbling soup.

"Liz?"

No answer again.

Panic struck her heart. There hadn't been food bubbling on the stove when she'd arrived home the night she'd discovered Burn and Layla in the garage. But she had walked into a silent home when she'd been expecting to enter a house filled with the noises of a toddler and her overworked dad.

Terrified now, she pivoted and would have raced back to the bedrooms, but as she turned, Darius came out of her bedroom, Gino on his arm.

"Sorry."

Her heart stopped. Her brain turned to mush. Intense relief flooded her, but before it fully registered, the sight of Darius turned her knees to rubber and her heart to a swampy pool of emotion. He looked tired. Awful. His hair went in four different directions. He hadn't shaved—for days, she would guess from the growth on his chin and cheeks.

"Don't worry. I showered."

His comment was so unexpected that a laugh burst from her chest. But she caught it after one quick giggle. This man had hurt her. True, it was partially her fault—okay, mostly her fault for assuming things he'd never said—but she didn't want to get hurt again. She wanted to recover. Which meant he couldn't simply come into her home and take over the apartment.

"I thought you were supposed to call and arrange visits?"

"I did. I called Liz. She actually needed some time to go to the library. She was happy I could watch Gino this afternoon."

"You've been here all afternoon?"

"And I brought soup from Cook as a peace offering." He strolled a little farther into the apartment. "She also gave me a pan of lasagna for tomorrow."

Her mouth watered, but she caught herself. Even if his motivation was good—happy, healthy Gino sat on his arm like a contented angel—and he'd brought food, she couldn't pretend everything was okay between them. Yes, she knew eventually she had to get along with him. But it was too soon. She wanted the time to heal, and by God she was taking it.

"I'm sorry, but—"

"Nick suggested I bring roses," he said, talking over her as he walked to the stove. He winced. "Thank you for catching the chowder before it boiled over. I'm not good at cooking."

He winced again. "My mom would be so mad that I forgot everything she taught me." He produced a small piece of paper. "Cook wrote out instructions for how to heat the lasagna tomorrow."

It finally struck her that he intended to be here tomorrow and righteous indignation roared to life inside her. Her heart hardened. She would not let this man worm his way into her life when she needed time to heal.

"Oh, no. No. No. No. You are not tricking me into letting you live here for the next year. I left Montauk for a good reason—"

"I know." He interrupted her tirade and came a little closer.

Her heart rate sped up. The breath in her lungs shivered. Every nerve ending in her body rose to the top of her skin and all but glowed with awareness. Still, her heart was hard, her determination to get over him strong. If he thought he was going to touch her and have her turn to putty in his hands—

He passed her and she spun around to see him sliding Gino into the swing behind her.

Color bloomed on her cheeks. Why couldn't her hormones realize this man didn't want her? Why did they always jump to wrong conclusions with him?

He faced her. His words were soft and

sincere when he said, "I am sorry for hurting you."

Her heart melted a tiny bit. There was nothing wrong with accepting a sincere apology from a guy she had to deal with for the next eighteen years. But she also had to take care of herself. She couldn't let him work his way too far into her life or her good graces.

"That's okay. I—"

"It wasn't okay." This time when he stepped closer, she saw the hesitation in his approach.

Her head tilted in fascination. She'd never seen him fearful before. Even when he'd never in his life as much as held a baby, he'd jumped in and tried things with Gino. To see him wavering now was odd, a curiosity.

"I am so bad at this because I have never done anything remotely like it before."

Her heart melted a bit more. She'd loved him because he was strong, but she also loved him for his honesty. And right now that honesty was costing him. How could she not melt a little inside?

"I love you."

That took her so much by surprise that her heart totally stopped, her chest seized, her mouth fell open.

"I thought I couldn't love." He snorted a

laugh. "I thought I was like my dad." He met her gaze. "Turns out I'd just never met the right woman."

She swallowed.

"Nick told me all this." He glanced at her. "He was married, you know? She left him. He told me I have all the symptoms of a broken heart, but that I was lucky." He sucked in a breath. "He thinks it isn't too late for me to apologize and ask for a second chance."

"Second chance?"

"We had a bad first chance. I did everything wrong."

"I wasn't exactly Mary Sunshine."

She saw the spark of hope blossom in his dark eyes.

"You're agreeable?"

"You did say you loved me."

"So much my heart hurts."

She laughed. He opened his arms and she stepped into them. Giddy joy flooded her. Relief felt like a warm blanket. Tears welled in her eyes. She'd never believed she would feel this again. Never believed life would be so kind as to give her a second chance. But it was. A chance fresher, brighter, better even than her first, because she now knew the fragility of life upped the importance of real love.

She'd never take him for granted.

"So isn't there something you want to say to me?"

She leaned back so she could look into his eyes. "I forgive you."

"Thanks, but I was hoping for something a little better than that."

"Better than forgiveness?" she asked, teasing him because she still needed a bit of reassurance that this wasn't a dream or a trick, and that they weren't misinterpreting their situation again.

"A lot better than forgiveness. Something that stands the test of time, means we'll be there for each other…means we'll raise Gino together."

She blinked. Shock and joy crashed in her heart. "Are you asking me to marry you?"

"Depends. Are you going to tell me what I need to hear?"

Her lips trembled. She smashed them together. She refused to cry—didn't want to cry. This was without a doubt the happiest moment of her life, the precipice of a new beginning, a second chance at everything, not just love, but babies, a soul mate, a home…an adventure.

She sucked in her breath, raised to her tiptoes, and said, "I love you, too, as her lips met his."

EPILOGUE

THE WEDDING TOOK PLACE in June at the house in Montauk. Darius's two brothers stood up for him as groomsmen. Whitney's two closest friends were at her side. She wore white—a simple strapless silk dress that caressed her curves—and carried roses. Her blond hair had been piled into a careless stack of curls on top of her head with tiny roses scattered between the loops.

Liz and Jake sat in the front row with her parents. Gino arched from her mom to Liz and back to her mom again until he realized Darius and Whitney were only a few feet away from him. Then he screeched and howled until the preacher stopped the service.

Darius laughed. "I'll get him."

He took the few steps over to Whitney's mom, and Gino all but flew into his arms. At nearly a year old, he was a handful, especially when he preferred walking to being held. Dressed in a little tux that matched those of Darius and his brothers, Gino easily could have been the most handsome brother.

Except to Whitney there was no one more handsome, more attractive, more wonderful than Darius. As she thought that, tears filled her eyes, but Gino picked that precise moment to launch himself at her. She caught him just in time.

The hundred or so guests in the ballroom of the Montauk house laughed.

Darius turned to the crowd. "Does anybody have a cookie?"

Mrs. Tucker bounced out of her chair. Wearing a pretty yellow suit, with her hair tucked into a French twist, she looked more like an aunt than his house manager. She produced a cookie from her suit pocket.

"I'm always prepared."

The crowd laughed again. Gino took the cookie and Darius settled the little boy on the crook of his arm.

"We can go on now."

The preacher smiled. Whitney slid her hand into the crook of Darius's elbow. The papers had been filed for Whitney and Darius to adopt Gino. They'd no longer be custodians, but parents. As Gino contently munched on his cookie, Whitney and Darius said the vows that officially made them man and wife.

Gino's parents.

Gerry and Julia Ross's daughter and son-in-law.

Nick and Cade's brother and sister-in-law.

A family.

Darius would never spend another Christmas alone.

LARGER-PRINT BOOKS!

GET 2 FREE LARGER-PRINT NOVELS PLUS
2 FREE GIFTS!

⬦ Harlequin

Romance

From the Heart, For the Heart

YES! Please send me 2 FREE LARGER-PRINT Harlequin® Romance novels and my 2 FREE gifts (gifts are worth about $10). After receiving them, if I don't wish to receive any more books, I can return the shipping statement marked "cancel." If I don't cancel, I will receive 6 brand-new novels every month and be billed just $4.34 per book in the U.S. or $4.99 per book in Canada. That's a saving of at least 16% off the cover price! It's quite a bargain! Shipping and handling is just 50¢ per book in the U.S. and 75¢ per book in Canada.* I understand that accepting the 2 free books and gifts places me under no obligation to buy anything. I can always return a shipment and cancel at any time. Even if I never buy another book, the two free books and gifts are mine to keep forever.

186/386 HDN FC9H

Name   (PLEASE PRINT)

Address   Apt. #

City   State/Prov.   Zip/Postal Code

Signature (if under 18, a parent or guardian must sign)

Mail to the **Reader Service:**
IN U.S.A.: P.O. Box 1867, Buffalo, NY 14240-1867
IN CANADA: P.O. Box 609, Fort Erie, Ontario L2A 5X3

Not valid for current subscribers to Harlequin Romance Larger-Print books.

**Are you a current subscriber to Harlequin Romance books
and want to receive the larger-print edition?
Call 1-800-873-8635 or visit www.ReaderService.com.**

* Terms and prices subject to change without notice. Prices do not include applicable taxes. Sales tax applicable in N.Y. Canadian residents will be charged applicable taxes. Offer not valid in Quebec. This offer is limited to one order per household. All orders subject to credit approval. Credit or debit balances in a customer's account(s) may be offset by any other outstanding balance owed by or to the customer. Please allow 4 to 6 weeks for delivery. Offer available while quantities last.

Your Privacy—The Reader Service is committed to protecting your privacy. Our Privacy Policy is available online at www.ReaderService.com or upon request from the Reader Service.

We make a portion of our mailing list available to reputable third parties that offer products we believe may interest you. If you prefer that we not exchange your name with third parties, or if you wish to clarify or modify your communication preferences, please visit us at www.ReaderService.com/consumerschoice or write to us at Reader Service Preference Service, P.O. Box 9062, Buffalo, NY 14269. Include your complete name and address.

The series you love are now available in

LARGER PRINT!

The books are complete and unabridged—
printed in a larger type size to make it
easier on your eyes.

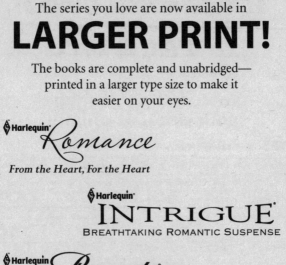

Harlequin *Romance*

From the Heart, For the Heart

Harlequin
INTRIGUE
BREATHTAKING ROMANTIC SUSPENSE

Harlequin *Presents*

Seduction and Passion Guaranteed!

Harlequin *Super Romance*

Exciting, emotional, unexpected!

Try **LARGER PRINT** today!

Visit: www.ReaderService.com
Call: 1-800-873-8635

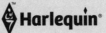

Harlequin®

A *Romance* FOR EVERY MOOD™

www.ReaderService.com

HLPDIR11